Curse of the Witch

Crypt Witch cozy paranormal mystery series - book 4

K.E. O'Connor

K.E. O'Connor Books

CURSE OF THE WITCH

Copyright © 2021 by K.E. O'Connor

ISBN: 978-1-915378-02-6

Written by: K.E. O'Connor

Chapter 1

I stretched my legs under the oak kitchen table and leaned back in my seat. I yawned loudly and gave a grateful nod as Mom placed a large mug of black coffee in front of me.

She sighed and shook her head, a mournful look on her face. "I just cleaned this kitchen floor." My dusty, gooey footprints led in from the hallway.

I took a long sip of coffee. "Sorry, I needed some downtime after finishing work and knew the perfect place to come." I patted the demon catching bag hanging from my black belt loop. It carried a particularly pesky demon I'd been tracking outside Willow Tree Falls for three long, stressful days. He'd not come quietly, but they rarely did. This spiteful demon had also showered me in bright green slime as he'd fought to stay out of my bag.

"You can also blame me for the visit," Wiggles said from his seated position by my knee. "I heard you were baking some peach cobblers. That's my favorite. Cora, you make the best cobbler."

I grinned at him. So long as it was sweet, it was Wiggles' favorite food. My hellhound had such a sweet tooth.

"You're right. I am making cobbler," Mom said. "There's none for you. It's for the party."

I tilted my head, hoping I'd not forgotten anyone's birthday. "Whose party?"

"Don't tell me it's not on your calendar." Mom smiled. "It's the highlight of your auntie's year."

I straightened in my seat. "It's not her birthday, is it?"

Mom flapped a dishcloth at me. "Of course it isn't. It's the thirtieth reunion of your auntie's biker gang. They're all arriving. In fact, she's out right now collecting two of them."

I sipped more coffee, slowly relaxing now I was home and safe, and no demon was trying to gouge my favorite body parts. I had forgotten about the reunion party. Auntie Queenie used to run with the Dead Tree Witch biker gang. The gang was a force to be reckoned with in Willow Tree Falls, but that was a long time ago. They had a reunion every year and made a special effort every ten years to celebrate the trouble they'd gotten into over the decades.

"She's been looking forward to this for months."

"Auntie Queenie will have a great time. It's the rest of us who'll suffer," I said.

Mom chuckled as she checked the contents of the oven. "It's only right your auntie gets to blow off steam now and again."

"It's how much steam she blows off that's the problem. Do you remember their twentieth anniversary reunion? They destroyed the fountain outside the mayor's house."

Mom twisted her mouth to the side. "It wasn't so much destroyed as permanently altered."

"Fountains aren't supposed to spurt flames!"

Mom laughed. "I do remember the mayor's face when he woke the next morning to find rivulets of fire dripping from his mermaid's urn."

"They never confessed to it, but it had to be them."

"She's promised they'll all be on their best behavior. And they're getting on a bit, so I can't imagine they'll be too much trouble."

Auntie Queenie was Mom's older sister, but she wasn't that old. She was in her late fifties but acted like a woman half her age.

"I hope I'm like the gang when I'm that age." They still acted like excited teenagers most of the time.

"I'm sure you will be. Although, the last time they met, Bastille complained of a lingering throat infection, and Samantha mentioned a sore hip. We can all be young at heart even when the body starts to misbehave."

Dodgy hips or not, these witches were a handful. But their parties were always great, and they were fun to hang out with, always telling incredible stories about what they got up to when they were in the gang.

"We're back!" Auntie Queenie called from the hallway. She bustled into the kitchen, a big smile on her face. Behind her were Esmeralda DuPont and Lila Beaumont.

Esmeralda was tall, thin, and pale with a sharp face and jet-black hair that I was certain she dyed.

Lila was a few years older and had a shock of ice-white hair that sat around her head in a fluffy cloud. She always had a smile on her plump face and a twinkle in her blue eyes.

Mom hurried over and hugged them both. "I hope you had pleasant journeys."

"Mine was fine." Esmeralda kissed her cheek and smiled at me.

"I can't understand why you don't remain in Willow Tree Falls all the time," Auntie Queenie said. She passed by my seat and ruffled the top of my hair.

"I love my commune too much," Lila said. "Us single witches need to stick together. The commune is a peaceful place, where we hone our skills and aren't bothered by others." Lila specialized in healing and water magic and had an affinity with the sea. Her commune was a short walk to a beautiful beach with long stretches of pristine sand and warm salt water pools you could bath in.

Auntie Queenie huffed as she took a bottle of brandy from the shelf and waved it in the air. "Is it too soon?"

"Not for me," Lila said.

"Lovely! I'll have some in my coffee," Esmeralda said as she took a seat at the table. "The old place hasn't changed. Queenie walked us around before we came here."

"It's the same as always." Auntie Queenie passed around large brandies and coffee. "You're still in that drafty old cottage on the moors?"

Esmeralda nodded. "It's not drafty. It's cozy. I get no interference from other people."

"It must get lonely out there on your own." Mom settled at the table with everybody and placed a plate of homemade chocolate chip cookies in the center.

"I'm actually thinking about downsizing," Esmeralda said as she took a cookie.

"There's always a place for you in Willow Tree Falls," Auntie Queenie said. "It could be like old times if you come back."

"My knees won't take kindly to riding on a bike," Esmeralda said. "I have trouble getting my leg over these days."

Lila snorted coffee across the table. "So do I!"

The three women cackled with laughter.

"You can ride pillion with me," Auntie Queenie said as she topped up the glasses.

Lila chuckled. "That would be a sight. Two aging biker chicks raising hell in Willow Tree Falls."

"Less of the aging," Auntie Queenie said. "I've got plenty of good years in me."

I sat back and listened to their good-natured banter. It was always the same when the gang got back together. It seemed like no time had passed. They were quick to catch up with recent news and then spent the rest of the time reminiscing about the good old days when their gang ruled Willow Tree Falls.

"You need to watch what you say." Auntie Queenie lifted her chin in my direction. "Tempest is in with the enemy these days."

I frowned at her. "What do you mean?"

"She's dating Rhett Blackthorn." Auntie Queenie's voice lowered to a conspiratorial whisper.

"That gang is still around." Esmeralda sniffed in disapproval. "Maybe we should re-form and run them out of the village once and for all."

"It's a different crew these days," Auntie Queenie said. "Tempest's dating the leader."

I waved a hand in front of my face. "It's early days with Rhett. You can say whatever you like in front of me. It won't get back to him." It had been three months since I'd helped rescue Rhett from a curse. A curse that almost killed him. After his brush with death, I realized I had strong feelings for him and wanted to see where our relationship went. So far, it had gone well. We'd been on numerous dates, and I enjoyed his company. The kissing wasn't bad either.

But we were taking it slowly. I wasn't letting the fact my heart beat fast whenever I was around him affect my judgment. And I had history with Rhett and a pesky demon living inside me who stirred up trouble at inappropriate times. Dating was difficult when you came with a dark shadow, but Rhett was understanding.

"We'll make sure not to talk about our revenge plots against Rhett and his gang." Lila winked at me.

"Talk away. That gang can be trouble, but they're mainly harmless."

"It used to be a much rougher crowd," Auntie Queenie said.

"So bad they ran us out of the village," Esmeralda said.

There were disapproving mutters from Auntie Queenie and Lila about that unfortunate truth.

"I'm sure they used underhanded tactics," Auntie Queenie said. "And they caught us at a weak moment. Only cowards do that."

Mom tactfully cleared her throat. She'd seen many times how angry Auntie Queenie and her former gang members got when they discussed losing their place in Willow Tree Falls. "What plans have you got to celebrate this year?"

"We're having a party in the forest," Auntie Queenie said. "I've cleared it with Suki and Fallon. They're fine with it so long as we don't cause any damage and put out the fire."

Suki and Fallon were the wood nymphs who looked after our forest. It wasn't any old forest. It was full of magic and used to store powerful magical items that were best kept out of people's way because of their destructive qualities.

"I've ordered plenty of food from Bite Me," Auntie Queenie said.

"I'm glad we're going sophisticated this time," Esmeralda said. "I'm not a fan of pizzas and hotdogs like you provided last time."

"I always say you can do the catering if you don't like it," Auntie Queenie said. "I thought we'd have something with a bit of pizzazz, given it's been thirty years since we got together."

The three women all looked at each other and grinned like excited school kids.

"It doesn't seem like more than a few years since we were all here," Lila said. "How can time go so fast?"

Esmeralda leaned forward, her eyes sparkling. "I've still got my bike in storage. I can't part with the old girl, even though I don't ride anymore."

"You should have brought her with you," Auntie Queenie said. "It would have been great to take her for a spin for old times' sake."

"You're not allowed to ride," Mom said. "Our magic barrier can only sustain so many hits."

Auntie Queenie clicked her tongue against the roof of her mouth. "That was an accident. I don't know why people bring that up. I can still ride if I have to."

"What's that you've got in your bag?" Lila pointed to the demon bag that hung from my belt.

"Tempest is still doing freelance demon hunting work for the angels," Auntie Queenie said. She nodded at my bag. "Have we got company?"

"We have but not for long," I said. "I only got back a few hours ago. I needed to recharge my batteries before facing the angels."

"Have you got anyone interesting in there?" Lila leaned closer, her eyes glistening with interest.

"No one you'd like to meet," I said. "He's a sneaky one. He had me on the run for three days before I tracked him to a back alley behind an exotic dance bar."

Auntie Queenie shook her head. "What is it with these demons? They're either obsessed with girls dancing in sparkly thongs or lurking around takeout places. You'd think they'd have better things to do, like try to take over the world. But no, all they're interested in is fast food and fast women."

"Which is handy for me," I said. "I know where to look, and I can grab some food after I've captured them."

"Let me take a peek," Lila said. "I haven't had a rumble with a demon for years." Her hand inched toward the bag.

"Best if we don't let a demon loose in Mom's kitchen." I kept a tight hold on the bag.

"I'll smack him down if he makes a scene." Lila's hand moved closer.

Mom jumped up and hurried to my chair, placing a barrier between me and Lila. "Tempest, it's time you left. You've got that demon to deal with, and you must get cleaned up before you meet Caprice, Samantha, and Bastille."

I slid her a sideways glance. I was grateful for the rescue from Lila's inquisitive hand but hadn't realized I was getting lumbered with collection duties for the rest of Auntie Queenie's gang. "Can't they find their own way here?"

Mom pulled my chair back and shooed me toward the door. "No, that's not polite. You meet them at the barrier and show them to the hotel."

"Someone needs to keep an eye on them," Auntie Queenie said. "Those three are trouble when they get together."

"We'll see you at the party." Mom ushered me into the hallway.

I stopped when we were by the door and out of earshot of the others. "What gives? Why are you so keen to get me out of here?"

Mom glanced over her shoulder. "Lila loves demons."

"She does?"

"The last time they were here, I caught her snooping around the cemetery, looking for a crack. She wanted to meet a demon, test her skills, and make sure they hadn't gotten rusty. I was worried she'd let out that demon you're carrying. I can't have that. He might destroy my peach cobblers."

I arched an eyebrow. "That would be a crime."

"It absolutely would." Wiggles wandered out of the kitchen, his mouth full of something that looked suspiciously like peach cobbler.

Mom tilted her head and tutted. "Go on. Get out of here you two. And wipe some of that goo off your clothes, or they'll think I raised a wildling."

I looked down and shrugged as I saw the stains on my outfit. "It's a part of the job."

"Your auntie's friends will think I don't look after you properly."

I kissed her cheek. "Mom, I can take care of myself. What time do I need to meet the rest of auntie's party?"

Mom checked the time and gasped. "Five minutes! They're arriving by the Green Man."

"Then I'd better get a move on." I hurried out of the house with Wiggles. There was no time for a change of clothes or clean-up of any kind. They'd have to take me as they found me. It wouldn't be the first time they'd seen me smeared in some kind of gross demon residue.

Wiggles trotted along beside me as I broke into a jog. "I love Queenie's reunions. They always know how to party."

"You only love them because they give unlimited belly rubs," I said.

"They have their priorities right," Wiggles said. "Party hard, treat a hellhound right, and have fun."

"Let's make a quick detour. I need to dump this demon before we meet the others just in case they get interested in trying to set him free, as well."

We changed direction and jogged to Angel Force's headquarters. It was a huge, white building in the center of the village.

I pushed through the door to find Dazielle at the desk, talking to Cassiel.

"One demon, all yours." I unclipped the bag from my belt and handed it to Dazielle.

"Good work." She passed the bag to Cassiel, who vanished out the back to decant him into a safe container. "I hear your auntie's having a party tonight."

"Good news spreads fast. Don't be offended if your invitation got lost in the post." Dazielle had a habit of accusing Auntie Queenie of things she hadn't done, and there was no love lost between them.

Dazielle smirked. "Tell her to be careful. I know what she's like."

"She knows how to have fun. There's nothing wrong with that."

"Even so, keep an eye on her and her misbehaving friends. I don't need a bunch of overexcited, middle-aged witches causing havoc in Willow Tree Falls."

"There might be a little havoc, but I'll see if I can keep a lid on things."

Cassiel returned and handed me my now empty bag.

"Make sure you do," Dazielle said. "I'll arrest them for disorderly conduct if things get out of hand."

"That'll look good in the local paper: *Police Chief Harasses Overexcited Middle-Aged Witches Reunion Shocker!!!*"

Dazielle sniffed. "I'll treat them the same as anyone else if they break the law."

"You should come to the party," Wiggles said, "so long as you promise not to be a party pooper. I'll see if I can get you in."

"I have better things to do than hang out with a bunch of eccentric witches," Dazielle said.

"Washing your hair?" I asked.

Her eyes narrowed. "Maybe. But I might drop by to make sure they aren't causing problems."

"We look forward to it. If you're bringing nibbles, we're low on salty snacks." I shook my head as we headed out of the building. Auntie Queenie would not want any angels at her party ruining the vibe.

I raced to the edge of the magic barrier where a broken hunk of green stone, known to locals as the Green Man, rested against a lightning struck oak.

I was just in time to see three women emerge. Their images looked misty as they passed through the magic.

Samantha Smythe-Barrow was easy to spot. She was a curvy witch with flame red hair and green eyes. She carried her fifty-five years well and often caught men's attention.

Bastille Drew was next. She'd always been the quiet one of the group. She had a neat gray bob, a fondness for long cardigans, and lots of silver rings.

Caprice Gray was the final arrival, with a neat dark pixie cut, a willowy figure, and intense dark eyes.

They all waved at me as I approached.

"Tempest, it's lovely to see you." Samantha air kissed either side of my cheeks. She was the refined one of the group until she'd had a few drinks.

"We've been so looking forward to our visit," Caprice said. "Where's Queenie?"

"Entertaining Esmeralda and Lila," I said. "She asked me to take you to the hotel."

"Lovely, and you must join us later on." Caprice grabbed my elbow and walked alongside me. "We're going to have such fun."

"I'll definitely drop by," I said.

"You must stay all night," Caprice said. "I want to hear all your news."

"Watch out. I spot trouble." Samantha grabbed Caprice and Bastille's arms and yanked them to a stop, her gaze narrowing as she stared across the street.

I looked over to where she was staring, and my eyes widened. Rhett and his entire gang sat astride their bikes in a single line of leather-clad menace. They hadn't been there when I'd hurried past a moment ago.

"If they're trying to intimidate us, it's failing." Caprice lifted her chin and stared them down. "They're little boys on big bikes that they don't know how to handle."

"They're fine," I said. "Give me a minute, though, and I'll make sure they're not after anything."

"They'll find my foot whacking them in the backside if they spoil our fun," Caprice hollered, loud enough so they could all hear.

I hurried over to Rhett, hoping the blush I felt hadn't spread to my cheeks. "You look like you mean business."

"Just making sure our new arrivals are appropriately welcomed." Rhett grinned at me and winked.

"Your gang rivalry was a long time ago, before you were head of this gang," I said.

"It's tradition when former gang members arrive in the village. It never hurts to remind them who's in charge," Rhett said. "We might be the new generation, but old grudges stick."

I shook my head. "Look at them. They're middle-aged women. They—"

"Incoming!" Josh yelled.

Rhett grabbed me and yanked me against his chest as something hot and magic-laced shot past us.

"Sorry!" Samantha shouted. "My aim's a little off."

I peered over Rhett's shoulder to see a flaming purple rock behind us. I turned toward her. "A little! You almost took my head off."

"See what I mean?" Rhett brushed my dark hair off my face, amusement glinting in his eyes. "They might have a few wrinkles, but those witches have power. They're not our fans, so we return the favor."

I nodded, my attention shifting to his mouth. "They won't be a problem. They're only here for a couple of days."

"They might be. Those witches have a lot of power, especially when they get together." Rhett's gaze moved over my shoulder, and his fingers tightened on my back.

I turned to see Caprice shoot a green flame into the air, her glare fixed on the gang.

I groaned and rubbed my forehead. "Okay, so they're powerful witches. They still won't cause you any trouble. They're here to get merry, drink too much, and talk about old times."

Rhett scrubbed his stubbled chin before nodding. "Are we still on for tomorrow night?"

I grinned at him. "Of course. Tonight, I have to take care of this lot, but I'm free tomorrow." Rhett had asked to take me stargazing. I wasn't sure I'd enjoy it, but if it meant alone time with Rhett, snuggled on a blanket, I was willing to experiment.

"I'll pick you up at ten. We won't get the best view until midnight."

"Not a problem." I glanced at the other members of his gang, who were watching the three witches with scowls on their faces, before giving him a quick kiss. "See you tomorrow."

I felt the urge to skip as I hurried away from Rhett. It was silly, but he always made me feel like a teenage girl with a giant crush.

Caprice shot another bout of flame into the air, and Samantha and Bastille laughed as I drew near.

I doused the flames with my own magic. "That's enough showing off."

Caprice raised her neat eyebrows at me. "You're having a dalliance with Rhett Blackthorn?"

I shrugged. "Sort of."

"What does Queenie think about that?" Samantha asked.

"If I'm happy, she's happy. Do you have an issue with who I date?"

Samantha laughed. "When he's as hot as that, of course not. It's just a shame he runs that rabble."

I turned and smiled at Rhett. "They aren't so bad when you get past the attitudes."

"I'm itching to try out my new ice spell," Caprice said. "I should see if these big, tough guys fancy a little frost on their beards."

"No! No frost on anything." I blew out a breath. "Let's get to the hotel."

"Just a little spell," Caprice said. "I promise not to hurt any of them." Ice danced across the ground toward the bikers.

"Wiggles." I pointed at the ice.

He sucked in a breath and belched out a hot steam of brimstone laced smoke, melting the ice.

"Oh, you're no fun, you bad puppy." Caprice pouted.

Wiggles shrugged. "I had trapped wind. If I hold it in, I get a stomach ache."

Caprice frowned. "I'm still keeping an eye on that gang. I don't trust them."

"No one does." I tilted my head in the direction of the hotel. "Let's get a move on. You don't want to be late for the fun."

These witches might be retired from the gang, but they were still a big handful of mischief.

Chapter 2

The mission I'd been forced into accepting by Mom that evening was to keep Auntie Queenie and her gang of delinquent buddies in line. If none of them got arrested and ended up in the angels' cells, I'd consider it a win.

After depositing Auntie Queenie's friends at the hotel, I'd headed to Cloven Hoof for a quick shower and a change of clothes. It was never polite to go to a party stinking of demon.

I now sat by an open fire in the forest with two forkfuls of melting marshmallows in my hands.

All of Auntie Queenie's friends sat around the fire, drinking spiced red wine from fancy gold chalices and chatting about old times. Nearly everyone from the family was here. The only ones missing were Grandpa Lucius and Uncle Kenny, who were at the cemetery keeping an eye on the demons.

I passed a fork of melted marshmallows to Aurora, who sat beside me, dressed in a fluffy white jacket and knee-high black boots, her hair hidden under a woolen hat.

She scooped off a finger of gooey marshmallow and blew on her finger. "That's hot!"

"Fire tends to make things warm. You should wait until they've cooled."

"No way." Aurora squashed the gooey marshmallow between two chocolate cookies before taking a bite and handing me half.

We both looked over and smiled as Auntie Queenie roared with laughter and slapped Lila on the back.

"She's still got it," Aurora said. "I hope we're like her when we're her age."

"Crazy, drinking too much brandy, and reading inappropriate books about how to spice up your love life?"

Aurora laughed. "Exactly. It'll be me and you, drunk, half-mad, and reading smutty novels. I can't wait."

That did sound like fun. I thought about Frank, and some of my happiness faded. He was behaving himself and had barely stirred all evening, even when Aurora sat next to me with a bag of marshmallows and two toasting forks. Would I still have a demon living inside me when I was Auntie Queenie's age? Maybe he wouldn't let me live that long.

I shook my head. It was no time for maudlin thoughts. This was a party, and I was determined to enjoy myself.

Wiggles bounced around between everyone, accepting belly rubs and treats whenever he could. He loved nothing more than a good party.

"Look out. We've got company." Lila jumped to her feet, her eyes narrowed.

I squinted through the gloom into the trees. Two shadowy figures stood outside the light of the fire. I tensed and rose slowly to my feet. Who would want to snoop on our party?

"Can you see who it is?" Aurora whispered.

"I'm not sure. They don't look friendly." I handed the other forkful of marshmallows to her and accessed my magic, sparking it on my fingers if I needed it in a hurry.

"You're not welcome here," Lila said sharply. "Get out before we run you out."

"Who is it?" Auntie Queenie joined her, along with Bastille.

"Two of those boys we saw when we arrived this afternoon," Samantha said. "I recognize the one on the left because of his ridiculous beard."

I sighed and shook my head. "I'll deal with this." Rhett's gang wouldn't be daft enough to come into the forest. They all knew what we were up to tonight. They must be looking for trouble if they were paying us a visit.

"You stay where you are. We've got this." Samantha and Caprice strode toward the bikers, sparks of yellow magic flaring from their fingers.

"There's no need for that." Alarm spilled through me as I saw the focused intent on the witches' faces.

They weren't playing around.

"Don't mind them. They're having fun," Auntie Queenie said as she settled back on her upturned log. "It's been awhile since any of us has gone up against the gang. It gets the juices flowing to have someone to battle with."

"It won't be fun if the fight gets serious," I said, my gaze not leaving Samantha and Caprice.

"Quick! They're making a run for it," Caprice said.

"Let's see if this puts them off of snooping on our fun." Samantha rolled a large ball of sparking electricity between her hands before flinging it after the retreating figures.

Two loud yelps and a torrent of angry curses filled the air as her magic made contact.

Samantha and Caprice laughed and clutched each other as they returned to their seats by the fire.

"You hit your targets," I said.

"I did. That was fun," Samantha said. "We must celebrate seeing off those rogues."

More wine was poured and chocolate covered buns passed around.

"We should start up the gang again," Esmeralda said. "I miss the fun we had."

"If my joints could take it, I'd be right behind you," Caprice said. "Every time I move these days, something aches."

"I've got an herbal remedy that might help," Aurora said. "It's good for aching joints."

Caprice patted her cheek, her face glowing, thanks to the wine. "You're such a sweet girl. I'll give it a try."

"Too much has happened since the gang broke up," Bastille said softly. "We've all changed."

"Speak for yourself," Auntie Queenie said. "I'm no different from when I was eighteen. I remember my first ride on a bike like it was yesterday. The wind in my hair and my skirt blowing up around my thighs. I'd never felt so free."

"You never wore a helmet." Bastille stared into the flames. "We all know why that is."

Auntie Queenie cocked her head, and her eyes narrowed. "Why don't you tell us just in case anyone's forgotten?"

I glanced at Aurora. I'd seen Auntie Queenie and Bastille bicker before. It was always over the same thing. Uncle Kenny.

"You wanted to catch a certain person's eye," Bastille said. "You thought he wouldn't notice you if you had a safety helmet on. And you used to wear those ridiculously short skirts on that bike. It's a wonder you weren't arrested for indecent exposure."

"Those skirts allowed me to move easily on the bike, and nothing stuck in the spokes," Auntie Queenie said. "There's nothing wrong with that."

"It made you look easy," Bastille said.

Auntie Queenie sucked in a breath, and her lips thinned.

"Now, now," Mom said. "You were young and enjoying yourselves. We've all got an inappropriate skirt in our closet."

"Bastille's still jealous," Aurora whispered. "You'd think she'd let it go after all these years."

I nodded. It was no secret that Uncle Kenny had dated Bastille before Auntie Queenie. They'd been together for six months when Queenie had caught his eye. He always said it was love at first sight. He saw her, and no other woman mattered. He always called her his beacon of light, although, perhaps the short skirt had helped.

Once they'd met, he'd ended things with Bastille. It was a long time ago, but Bastille had trouble letting go.

"Bastille never married," Aurora said quietly.

"She must have dated after Uncle Kenny," I said. "He's a lovely guy, but he's not the only lovely guy on the planet." To look at Uncle Kenny, you'd never think he was such a stud in his youth. He was quiet, polite, and reserved. A kind-hearted guy who always looked out for others and kept his head down and out of trouble.

"Maybe she thought he was her true love," Aurora said. "When you find it, you just know." She sighed and gazed at the stars.

Aurora was besotted by Toby Matlock. So far, she was still not telling anybody else about him but did keep dropping hints about them moving in together. Any day now, she'd have to come clean and let everyone know what she was doing. I'd make sure not to be around when that happened.

Grandpa Lucius strode through the forest toward the fire. He gave everyone a cheery wave as he looked around. "Having fun, ladies?"

Granny Dottie hopped up and kissed his cheek. "Of course. Don't tell me it's a shift change already. I was just getting going."

"Afraid so, old girl. The demons request the presence of your delightful company."

"Where's Uncle Kenny?" Aurora stood. She was joining Granny Dottie for a shift in the cemetery.

Grandpa Lucius rubbed the back of his neck. "He stayed behind. He didn't want things to get tense around here." He looked pointedly at Bastille.

"Understood," Granny Dottie said briskly. "There's no point in opening old wounds."

"Ancient wounds more like," I muttered. Bastille needed to get over having a crush on my uncle. It was sort of creepy.

"Come on." Granny Dottie linked arms with Aurora. "Let's go bash some misbehaving demons."

I said goodbye to them and settled back in my seat, soaking up the atmosphere and enjoying some delicious cobbler Mom had baked for the party.

Samantha looked around the group, a smile on her lips. "I just remembered the time we snuck into the thermal spas and dyed the water."

Caprice snorted a laugh. "It was the day before the mayor brought his fancy friends to visit."

Auntie Queenie roared with laughter. "After they had a dip, they came out purple."

I joined in the laughter as I ate my cobbler. This was what life was all about. Great friends, close family, and incredible desserts.

It wasn't until almost midnight when the party broke up.

All of Auntie Queenie's friends staggered away toward the hotel, while Mom and Grandpa Lucius did a quick clear up and made sure the fire was out.

Auntie Queenie leaned heavily on my shoulder as I helped her to her feet.

"Did you have a fun night?" I asked her.

"The best." She planted a sloppy kiss on my cheek. "Those girls are incredible. Absolutely nuts, but brilliant fun. When I'm with them, I know someone has my back. That was the incredible thing about being part of the gang. You knew you had someone looking out for you. No matter how bad things got, they were always there."

"It sounds awesome."

She hiccupped and giggled. "I might have had a bit too much wine."

I smiled. "Just a bit."

"It won't be many more years before I'm too old to party. I have to enjoy myself while I can."

"You know that's not true," I said. "You'll be partying long after I'm gone."

That comment earned me another kiss.

"Let's get you home," I said.

Mom loaded Grandpa Lucius with leftover food and empty dishes and sent him on ahead before grabbing Auntie Queenie's other arm and wrapping it around her shoulders. "You old lush. You're setting a bad example for Tempest and Aurora."

"It was a little fun," Auntie Queenie slurred. "My nieces are too sensible to follow my example."

Mom shook her head and looked at me. "This is not the way you're supposed to live your life."

"You said it yourself. There's no harm in letting off steam," I said.

"Toot, toot," Auntie Queenie said. "I feel like I'm all puffed out after tonight."

"I couldn't help but notice things got tense with Bastille."

Auntie Queenie waved a hand as if conducting an orchestra. "Take no notice of her. We both loved the same man, but I won him. There are no hard feelings. Bastille sees how happy Kenny makes me and how happy I make him." She started singing out of tune as we walked slowly back to the house.

Uncle Kenny opened the door as we arrived. He chuckled and shook his head. "Had a good night, beautiful?"

Auntie Queenie flung her arms around his neck and gave him a big smooch. "The best. You're the best. Have I ever told you I love you?"

"Only every day of our married life." He grinned at me and Mom. "I'll take it from here."

"Are you going to carry me up the stairs?" Auntie Queenie asked.

"Not unless you want me to put my back out," Uncle Kenny said as he guided her to the stairs. "That's it. One step at a time. We'll get there."

I stood at the bottom of the stairs with Mom until we were sure they weren't going to topple down in a drunken heap.

Mom walked into the kitchen and switched on the kettle. "Do you want a mug of cocoa before bed?"

"That sounds good." I curled my feet underneath me, and Wiggles settled by the chair, exhausted after his fun night of partying and food. "Bastille still seems hung up on Uncle Kenny."

"She took it hard when they got together." Mom made the cocoa and sat next to me at the table.

"They were only teenagers when they dated. She couldn't have expected it to last."

"She absolutely did," Mom said. "Your auntie makes light of it now, but they weren't friends for a long time. It was all because Kenny chose Queenie over Bastille."

"He didn't mess them around?" Uncle Kenny was the sweetest of guys. I couldn't imagine him fooling with people's emotions.

"No, your uncle was straight down the line. He was clear with Bastille. He said he cared for her, but he was in love with Queenie. Bastille tried to win him back and used several underhanded tactics. She even tried to get him drunk and seduce him."

"No way! Bastille's so quiet. You'd never think she was so devious by looking at her." I liked Bastille, but she'd always been a little stand-offish, not like the others who always wrapped me in warm hugs and gave me too many kisses.

"Bastille had a habit of asking Kenny out, just as a friend, and then trying to win him back."

I frowned. "I'm glad she failed."

"So am I. That's why your uncle stayed away from the party. He didn't want to upset Bastille. He'd like to be her friend, but it's not possible. And he'd hate to rub her nose in it if Bastille saw Queenie with him. For years after they were married, Bastille still wrote your uncle love notes, trying to convince him he'd made a mistake."

"That's plain weird," I said. "Six months in a relationship with Uncle Kenny, and she can't let him go. He's a nice guy, but…"

"Your uncle is a special guy," Mom said.

"Even so, that's unhealthy."

"It is. But suddenly, she stopped. I always figured Bastille had found someone else."

"But she never married."

"No, and I don't think she even dated. Bastille leads a quiet life. She stayed in the gang, but after moving out of Willow Tree Falls, she wasn't a regular. She'd drop in and out and keep in touch with the other members, but she was a part-time member. She found it too painful and didn't want to risk seeing Queenie and Kenny together and so obviously happy."

"It sounds like she needs to get a life," I said. "She has to have moved on by now."

"You'd think so. Speaking of moving on." Mom arched an eyebrow. "How are things going with you and Rhett?"

"Oh, you know, they're going." I downed my cocoa. If Mom was going to quiz me about my love life, it was time to leave.

"When can I expect him for dinner?"

"In about ten years."

She swatted the back of my hand. "Tempest, if he's going to be a significant part of your life, he needs to be a part of our family. We need to welcome him."

"You mean hassle him. Rhett's a new part of my life, and we're taking things slowly. You know it's not straightforward to date me."

"Even if you didn't have a demon living inside you, it wouldn't be straightforward. That doesn't mean I can't give your boyfriend a home-cooked meal now and again. I worry about those biker boys and what they eat. They always seem to be eating pizza."

"Tate makes a mean pizza. I could live off his pizza every day."

Mom tutted. "You tell Rhett that any time he wants a decent feed to come here. We'd all love to see him again."

"And by see him, you mean grill him about his intentions toward me and scare him off."

"There might be some gentle grilling." She stroked a strand of my dark hair off my face. "After all, I need to make sure you're treated well and looked after."

"You can be sure that, if Rhett ever mistreats me, it will be the last time I see him. I'm a big girl."

"You can be as big as you like. I'll always keep looking after you." Mom jumped up and wrapped two pieces of peach cobbler. "Take this with you, but don't eat it for breakfast."

I grinned at her. "As if I would."

She kissed my cheek as she walked me to the door.

Wiggles wandered along behind us, his nose in the air as he smelt the peach cobbler.

"I expect your auntie won't be up early tomorrow."

"From the amount of wine she drank tonight, it will be a miracle if she surfaces all week."

"It takes more than some spiced wine to knock her off her feet." Mom waved us goodbye as we headed out the door and into the quiet lane.

Tonight had been a lot of fun. I'd sort of failed in my mission to keep everyone in line, but it had been an enjoyable failure. And everyone, so long as I discounted Rhett's idiot gang members, had come out unscathed.

Wiggles nudged me with his nose as we walked back to Cloven Hoof. "Peach cobbler for breakfast?"

I grinned at him. "Of course. What other option is there?"

Chapter 3

I sat bolt upright in my bed, my heart racing.

Boom! Boom! Boom!

There it was. That noise hadn't been in my head.

Wiggles opened one eye and stared at me. "What is that?"

"I think it's a who. And whoever's banging on our door this early had better have a good excuse." The thudding came again. They weren't going away.

I reluctantly slid out of my cozy bed and shuffled to the door. I pulled it open, ready to give whoever dared invade my sleep a piece of my mind.

"Tempest! Something terrible has happened." Auntie Queenie stood in front of me, her hair a disheveled mess and her dressing gown on over her checked pajamas.

I caught hold of her hand, worry flooding through me as I saw she'd been crying. "What's the matter? It's not Mom? Is everything okay at home?"

She covered her mouth with her hand for a second. "It's Bastille. She's dead."

I gasped and wrapped Auntie Queenie in a tight hug. "Come in. You've had a shock." I was just as shocked. Bastille wasn't much older than Auntie Queenie. She was too young to die.

"No, I don't have time. I need to get back to the hotel." Auntie Queenie stepped away and scrubbed the tears off her cheeks. "I thought you could help me."

"Of course, whatever you need. Give me five minutes, and I'll come with you." I couldn't let Auntie Queenie go to the hotel alone. I gestured her into my apartment. "Do you know what happened?"

Auntie Queenie bit her bottom lip. "She was always a kind, quiet soul. She had a dark sense of humor that could offend if you didn't know her well, but she never meant anything by it. I can't believe this has happened."

"Of course you can't." I hugged Auntie Queenie again. I'd never seen her look so shocked. "Have you seen her? Did she die in her sleep?"

"No, nothing like that. I didn't get a good look at her body when I went to the hotel. I got a message on the snow globe from Tabitha to let me know what was going on."

Tabitha Dimples ran the hotel everyone was staying in. "So, what did happen?"

Auntie Queenie swallowed as a tear trickled down her cheek. "There's a possibility it was a demon attack."

My mouth fell open. "A demon loose in Willow Tree Falls. That's not possible. We'd know about it."

She clasped her hands together, her bottom lip trembling. "What if one escaped from the cemetery and we missed it?"

"There's not a chance of that. We don't mess around when we're on duty at the cemetery." My eyes narrowed as I looked at the guilty expression on her face. "Do we?"

Auntie Queenie looked away. "I can get caught up in my steamy romances. They're so distracting. I lose myself in them when I'm taking notes."

"Distracting enough that you'd let a demon sneak past?"

She sighed. "I hope not. What if it happened, though? I could have set a demon loose, and he killed my friend."

"No, this isn't your fault. If a demon so much as pokes his ugly head out of the prison, we know about it. This can't be a demon from our prison." At least, I hoped it wasn't, or we were in huge trouble.

Auntie Queenie wrung her hands together. "If it wasn't a demon, something awful happened to Bastille. It wasn't a natural death. The smell…" she looked away and wiped her cheeks with her fingers.

"Wait right here." I raced into the bedroom and threw on the first clothes I could find. "It's time to get up." I nudged Wiggles as I pushed my feet into my boots.

"What's going on?" he grumbled.

"Auntie Queenie's had a shock. We need to help her." I sorted through my laundry basket and found an over-sized black pullover.

Wiggles yawned and rolled off the bed. He stretched before trotting in front of me back into the living room. "What's up, Auntie Q?"

"Oh, Wiggles." She bent and wrapped him in a huge hug. "I'm in need of your nose."

He wriggled in her tight embrace and glared at me. "What do you need my nose for?"

Auntie Queenie stifled a sob. "To help my dead friend." She buried her nose in his fur.

"Let's go see what's happening at the hotel." I helped Auntie Queenie to her feet and handed her the pullover. "Put this on. It's chilly outside."

She looked at her clothes and laughed sadly. "I didn't even think about getting dressed when I heard the news. I raced straight to the hotel. I leaped right over your uncle, who was still sound asleep."

"Don't worry. We'll get this figured out." We left Cloven Hoof and hurried to the hotel. It was still early. The sun hadn't long been up, and there was a chill in the air.

Only a couple of stores were open, and I looked longingly at Brogan's cafe and wondered if I dared sneak in and grab a coffee. But Auntie Queenie was focused on getting to the hotel. My coffee would have to wait.

Auntie Queenie shook her head. "I'd planned to meet the girls for breakfast, make the most of the day while we're all here. Everyone will be devastated by what's happened."

"Who found Bastille?"

"Samantha. She's always been an early riser. She knocked on her door and found it open. There was no sign of Bastille inside. Samantha went out the back and found her."

"Where was she found?"

"Behind the hotel. Tabitha has a private garden for residents to use. Samantha ran in screaming. Tabitha called me and asked for my help."

"Was Bastille killed outside?"

"I don't know. I can't think clearly. That's why I came to get you. I knew you'd help. You're so good at puzzling things through. I don't know what she was doing outside."

"Maybe she went out to get some air if she couldn't sleep."

Auntie Queenie dabbed at her eyes. "Tempest, I'll never forgive myself if this happened because of me."

"Don't think like that. We need to find out what happened before we worry about the prison. It can't be one of our demons involved."

"I can't help it. Bastille didn't deserve this."

I watched as an angel descended from the sky and landed outside the hotel. "Angel Force has been informed?"

"Tabitha messaged them before making contact with me. They've sealed off the garden and are looking around. I overheard Dazielle mention demons, which is when I started panicking."

"What makes them think it was a demon?"

"Bastille's skin has been burned. It looks like she was grabbed and choked by someone with hot hands. Demon hot hands."

A shudder ran through me. This wasn't sounding good.

We reached the hotel where a small crowd was gathered at the front. Among them was Aurora and Granny Dottie.

I hurried over, keeping a tight hold of Auntie Queenie. "What are you doing here?"

"I was opening the store when I heard the news," Aurora said. "We had to come and see. Poor Bastille, this is horrible."

I nodded. "You both took the late shift at the cemetery last night. Were the demons acting up?"

"No," Aurora said. "It was quiet."

"No demons tried to get out or cause a distraction?"

Aurora's eyes widened. "I heard the angels mention demons. Did a demon kill Bastille?"

"We're not sure," I said.

"I am," Auntie Queenie whispered. "I got a glimpse of Bastille."

"I'm sure no demon escaped on our watch." Aurora's cheeks paled as she turned to Granny Dottie. "We didn't let anyone out, did we?"

"Absolutely not." Granny Dottie wrapped an arm around Aurora's shoulders. "We were there the whole time, and nothing stirred. There's no chance a demon crept out and did this to Bastille."

Samantha, Lila, Caprice, and Esmeralda hurried over, all looking as pale and shocked as Auntie Queenie.

The women all talked at the same time, comforting each other and hugging. Hankies were produced and shared to mop wet eyes and noses.

"Auntie Queenie, stay here with the others," I said. "I'll see what I can find out from the angels."

I left her with Aurora, Granny Dottie and the others and headed through the hotel to the back door and into the garden with Wiggles.

We were stopped by a large, blond, broad-shouldered angel, who peered down at me and fluttered his wings. "Nobody gets through. This is a crime scene."

"I can go through. I'm sort of a consultant," I said. I didn't recognize this angel. He must be a new recruit. He sure was an attractive one, if you liked your guys seven feet tall, muscled, and blue-eyed.

The angel's eyes narrowed. "I know who you are. Dazielle doesn't want anyone in until the scene has been examined."

"Is Dazielle here?" I tried to look past the angel but was blocked by a wall of white feathers.

"She is."

"Is there any chance I can have a word with her?"

"I'll see if she's available. Wait here." The angel walked away. He spoke to a colleague, who came closer, her attention on me.

I knelt next to Wiggles. "How do you fancy a sneaky look at the crime scene? See what happened to

Bastille."

Wiggles' eyes gleamed red. "I'd be happy to if you can provide the distraction so I don't get stomped by those horrors in white." He eyed the angels as they discussed me and shook their heads.

I walked over to them. The other angel was also new and just as attractive with long blonde hair, curves a guy would kill to touch, and big, blue eyes.

"What do you think happened?"

The angel eyed me with suspicion. "That's what we're trying to find out."

I stuck my hand out. "I'm Tempest Crypt. We've not met."

The angel nodded but didn't shake my hand. "Dazielle warned me about you."

"That's lovely to hear. Do you have a name?"

"I do."

This wasn't going well. It looked like I was in Dazielle's bad books again. I shifted to the right, and the angels matched my step just as I hoped they would. It meant Wiggles could sneak past unnoticed, which was exactly what he did.

"What theories do you have as to the cause of death?" I asked. "I heard a rumor it could be a demon."

The beautiful blond angel glanced at her colleague. "You shouldn't listen to rumors."

"Tempest!"

I looked past the mean angels to see the smiling face of my favorite cute but dumb angel, Dominic.

"Hey, Dominic. How's everything going?"

He grinned at me. "I'm not loving this early start, but other than that, things are good. How about you?"

"No complaints." I walked away from the grumpy angels and took Dominic with me. "What are you thinking happened here?"

Dominic scratched his head. "It's hard to say. The body's in a bad way. Whatever got her, it was something hot."

"Demon hot?"

The other angels, who were clearly listening in to our private conversation, cleared their throats.

Dominic glanced over his shoulder. "It could be. But you have a handle on all the demons. You wouldn't let one loose in Willow Tree Falls, would you?"

"Not a chance. Our prison is impenetrable. And if any were on the loose and causing trouble, you'd know about it."

"That's right, and we'd call you in to deal with it. We make a great team." His grin widened. He was the only angel I knew who was always happy to see me.

Shouts rang out in the garden, followed by the sounds of a scuffle. It looked like Wiggles had been discovered doing his undercover sleuthing. I hoped he'd had a chance to look around before he was caught.

Dominic turned and straightened his spine as Dazielle strode toward us. She had something wrapped in her wings, and I'd lay money on what it was.

"Tempest! You must control your hellhound." She opened her wings.

Wiggles dropped to the floor. He shook out his fur and scowled at Dazielle. "I was taking a morning walk. There's no crime in that."

"There is when you're deliberately nosing around a closed crime scene," Dazielle said. "And I know why you're doing that." She glared at me. "Keep him out of here."

"He was curious, as we all are. What do you think happened?"

Dazielle shook her head. "This one isn't for you."

"Was it a demon attack?"

Dazielle's eyes narrowed. "Most likely, but we need more time here before we can say for certain. Go home. There's nothing you can do." She stalked off.

I shrugged. "See you around, Dominic."

"Sure! Anytime you want to catch up over a drink, you just let me know."

I raised a hand in acknowledgement as I walked away with Wiggles. "What do you think happened?"

"It looks demon related to me," he said. "Bastille has burn marks around her neck. It looks like she was choked to death. Her skin is charred like overcooked barbecue chicken."

I wrinkled my nose. "Let's not mention the chicken reference to Auntie Queenie."

"She's already seen her. She knows how bad it is."

"Even so, she doesn't need the reminder. Bastille was her friend."

Wiggles nodded. "And the body is cold. Bastille's been dead for hours."

"Maybe she didn't even make it to bed. Bastille could have come back to the hotel and gone outside straightaway." But why would she do that? Something must have tempted her outside on a chilly evening.

I walked out the front of the hotel, back to where the others stood.

"What news?" Auntie Queenie asked.

"Not much. Dazielle wasn't all that helpful. Wiggles had a look around, but it's not looking good. It might be a demon."

Auntie Queenie shook her head. "A demon slaying in our village. I never thought I'd see such a horror."

"Let's go home," Granny Dottie said. "We've all had a shock. We need strong tea and something fortifying inside us."

"Good idea," Aurora said. "I'll make everyone breakfast."

"I can't eat," Auntie Queenie said. "But a cup of strong coffee will be good."

"Hold it right there." Dazielle strode over before we had a chance to leave. "Queenie, I need to take your statement as soon as possible. You were one of the first to find Bastille."

She nodded, her eyes wide and tear-filled. "Of course. If I can help, I will."

"We're going back to our house for breakfast," Granny Dottie said. "We'll take everyone with us, so we'll all be there when you want to take statements."

"No, that won't happen." Dazielle glared at the group. "Queenie and her friends are all suspects."

The group erupted, everyone protesting their innocence and talking over each other.

Dazielle raised a hand and waited for the shouting to die down. "This isn't up for discussion. You were all together last night. I need to speak with you separately to confirm alibis. Until I do that, you can't remain together."

"I thought Bastille was killed by a demon," Aurora said.

Dazielle pursed her lips. "It's possible but not definite. The evidence isn't conclusive. Until I know for certain what happened, you're all under suspicion."

This caused another flurry of objections.

"We're not going to spend the morning getting our stories straight if that's what you're worried about," I said.

Her eyes narrowed. "That's exactly what I'm worried about. Bastille was murdered. Until I determine your alibis, you stay apart. If I have to, I'll arrest you all and put you in separate cells so you can't talk. I'm hoping you'll be sensible enough not to force me to do that."

"What are we supposed to do while we wait for you to interview us?" Auntie Queenie asked.

"I suggest you go your separate ways. Everyone staying in the hotel needs to go to your room."

"That's not right. We'll be prisoners," Samantha said.

"No, you'll be making it easier for me to catch the killer," Dazielle said. "It won't take long, and this way is more comfortable."

"What about me and Tempest?" Auntie Queenie asked. "I can't lock myself in a room."

"Of course you won't," Granny Dottie said. "You're coming home. The angels can't object to that."

Dazielle hesitated, her suspicious gaze shifting from me to Auntie Queenie. "No discussing what happened."

"We won't mention it," Auntie Queenie said before nudging me.

Dazielle glared at me. "I'm serious. No talking about last night. You were both there as was the rest of your family. If I get a sniff you're hiding anything, I'll drag everyone in for questioning. I'll make sure the whole village sees you're under suspicion for murder."

Dazielle would be mean enough and dumb enough to do just that. "We're all innocent. And Bastille was a friend. No one in this group would hurt her."

"That's what I need to find out. I'll be in touch to take your statements."

After lots of hugging and promises to meet later, the group dispersed, and Auntie Queenie's friends headed into the hotel.

Auntie Queenie grabbed my hand. "Tempest, help me find out what happened to Bastille. I can't imagine any of my friends harming her, and it wasn't any of us, but someone wanted her dead."

I wrapped my arms around her. "Of course I'll help. I liked Bastille. We'll get whoever did this."

"And make them pay." Auntie Queenie squeezed me so tightly I worried a rib might crack. "We'll get them and teach them a lesson."

"Come on." Granny Dottie extracted me from Auntie Queenie's grip. "Let's get back to the house, and we can figure out this mess together."

I shook my head. "Why don't you and Aurora head to the cemetery? Check everything is okay with the prison."

"Good idea. We can't have those angels thinking our prison is not secure." Granny Dottie grabbed Aurora's hand, and they hurried toward the cemetery.

I kept hold of Auntie Queenie's arm as we walked away. I glanced over my shoulder to see Dazielle watching us.

I glared at her before turning away.

She thought she'd spotted a killer among us, but I'd prove her wrong. We were all innocent, but whoever had done this to Bastille would pay.

Chapter 4

I sat at the table in Mom's kitchen while she made strong tea laced with a shot of brandy for Auntie Queenie. A heap of buttered toast sat on the plate in the center of the table, but no one seemed hungry.

She'd been as shocked as everyone else when she'd learned what happened to Bastille, but she'd soon gone into caring mode and was fussing around everyone trying to get them to eat.

Auntie Queenie sat next to me, her hand clasped in mine.

"I loved Bastille," she said. "She was an odd fish at times, but she was still one of the gang."

"What made her odd?" I asked.

Auntie Queenie pulled at her bottom lip. "She liked to live in the past and had trouble letting go of things. She'd bring up conversations we'd had twenty years ago, recalling them like they were yesterday and we were just picking up where we left off."

"Especially when it came to Kenny," Mom said. "We all remember how obsessed Bastille was with him."

Auntie Queenie shook her head. "It was such a shame. Bastille was a real beauty when she was younger. She had long blonde hair and a twinkle in her eye. She enjoyed life and was always laughing. When Kenny left her, she changed."

"That's not your fault," I said. "You never chased after Uncle Kenny. He couldn't help who he fell in love with."

Auntie Queenie nodded. "I knew how much Bastille still cared for Kenny. She couldn't let go of the past. I felt a little sorry for her. It ruined her happiness. It ruined her chance to move on and be with somebody else."

"You never rubbed it in her face." Mom placed a plate of crumpets in front of us and poured more brandy before settling on the opposite side of the table.

"We were always discreet," Auntie Queenie said. "Bastille was heartbroken when they parted. We used to go on dates outside of Willow Tree Falls so she wouldn't stumble across us getting cozy in a restaurant. It made the relationship tricky, but I didn't want to hurt her more than she was already hurting."

"Bastille's death can't be connected to Kenny and how she felt about him," Mom said. "It's ancient history. Even though she wasn't happy about it, she'd accepted that you're together."

"It sounds like it took a long time for her to accept it, though," I said.

"Decades," Auntie Queenie said.

"What about her family?" I asked.

"She had no family. Bastille was an only child. Her parents are dead. She has no living relatives." Auntie Queenie sniffed and dabbed her nose. "She was all alone. Her death makes no sense."

"It made sense to someone," I said.

"Let's see what Aurora discovers at the cemetery," Mom said.

"It can't be one of our prisoners," I said.

"I know." Mom patted my hand. "We need to be doubly sure, and the angels will ask us to check. We'll ensure the place is sealed and nothing got out."

"What if a demon broke through the magic barrier around the village?" Auntie Queenie asked.

"We'd know about it. No one wants an unmonitored demon skulking about the village," I said.

"It won't do any harm for you to scout around," Mom said. "We must show willingness with the angels."

I shrugged. "I can look. We have to keep Dazielle and her angels off our backs. If they think for a second we're involved, they'll hound us."

Auntie Queenie sighed. "Which is why you must help, Tempest. We have to find the killer. We can't let those pretty feathery fools arrest the wrong person. Bastille deserves justice."

"I won't let that happen. Even though Dazielle doesn't want me involved, I'm not staying away. And you have nothing to worry about. Your alibi is solid," I said. "You were with me and Mom when we came back after the party. You were so merry, you could barely stand, let alone cast a working spell."

Auntie Queenie glared at me out of the corner of her eye. "I wasn't that bad."

Uncle Kenny bounded down the stairs, his eyes wide. "My love! You're back."

Auntie Queenie jumped up and hugged him. "Bastille's dead."

"I know." He wrapped his arms around her and tucked her head under his chin as he blinked tears out of his eyes. "Do you know what happened?"

She filled him in on the events of this morning. "The angels will question all of us."

"What nonsense. It wasn't any of us," Uncle Kenny said. "I know for a fact it wasn't you. After you collapsed into bed, you kept me awake most of the night with your snoring. I'd have known if you'd left because I'd have been able to sleep. You were with me all night."

"Of course I was, but I don't snore that loudly." Auntie Queenie returned to sit at the table.

Uncle Kenny joined us, the shock clear on his pale face. "Poor Bastille. She didn't deserve to go out that way. She was a gentle soul. She deserved so much better."

Aurora hurried through the doorway, Granny Dottie right behind her. "We've checked with Grandpa

Lucius, and everything's fine at the cemetery. All the demons are accounted for. There's no way one broke out and killed Bastille."

"I wish one of them had," Auntie Queenie said with a sigh. "It would mean we're all innocent. I can't believe any of my friends could do this to her."

"We still need to discount a demon on the loose in the village," Mom said. "At least we know our prison is secure."

"It's happened a few times, but it's been years since a demon has snuck in," Auntie Queenie said. "The magic around Willow Tree Falls is strong."

Which meant it was most likely someone in the village. Someone Bastille knew. I took hold of Auntie Queenie's hand. "I hate to ask, but out of your friends, who had a reason to want Bastille dead?"

Auntie Queenie shook her head. "None of them. Bastille used gentle magic and never dabbled with any shady stuff that got her noticed."

"She had no enemies that I know of," Uncle Kenny said. "She was a good sort and kept to herself. I can't imagine anyone who'd wish to do her harm."

"Somebody did, and it was someone who knew she'd be in Willow Tree Falls at the hotel last night. We have to consider everyone, and that includes the rest of Auntie Queenie's old biker gang."

"I can't think about it. It's not right. We look out for each other. Even though we're not in a gang anymore, we always will." Auntie Queenie swallowed and looked away.

"What if things have changed? You don't see so much of each other. Bastille could have fallen out with one of the others. Is there anyone in the group not close to Bastille?"

Auntie Queenie stifled a sob and shook her head.

"I know this is hard, my love," Uncle Kenny said. "But Tempest is trying to help."

Auntie Queenie sighed and patted my hand. "I know."

"It can be anything you think of. An argument you overheard or a cross word. I need something to get started with."

She nodded and straightened in her seat. "If I had to pick anyone, it would be Caprice. Bastille thought she was snooty and looked down on her. They often bickered, and Caprice would make fun of Bastille because she couldn't afford designer shoes. Caprice loves the finer things in life."

I frowned. "Caprice killed Bastille because she wouldn't wear designer clothes?"

Auntie Queenie tutted. "Of course not! And their bickering wasn't serious. They simply came from different backgrounds. And they'd always watch out for each other when we were together. If anyone else ever hassled Bastille, Caprice was there making sure they didn't do it again."

"Could their bond have faded over the years?" I asked. "Maybe Bastille got sick of being teased and confronted Caprice. Things got out of hand. You all had a lot to drink last night."

"Caprice wouldn't have killed Bastille."

"Caprice is a powerful witch," I said. "Is she powerful enough to burn another witch with magic?"

Auntie Queenie pressed her lips together. "In theory, but only in theory. None of them have anything to do with this."

"I believe you, but we need to cover all the bases. The angels will ask the exact same questions." I sat back in my seat. It wasn't much to go on, but it was a start.

Auntie Queenie looked at me, her bottom lip wobbling. "What are you going to do?"

"See if I can get to Caprice before the angels talk to her."

"Go easy on Caprice," Mom said. "She's most likely in shock. Everyone is."

"I'll ask a few questions, that's all. I need to rule her out and make sure they weren't arguing about something more complicated than designer shoes."

"She's innocent," Auntie Queenie said. "We all are."

"And that's what I'm going to prove." I nodded to Wiggles as I stood and walked to the kitchen door. "I will find out who did this. I won't stop asking questions until I do. We'll get justice for Bastille."

Auntie Queenie's smile was tearful as I turned and left the kitchen. It was time to investigate this murder and figure out who hated Bastille enough to kill her.

Chapter 5

I slowed as I saw feathers drifting in the air currents. There were angels around somewhere, and those feathers were suspiciously close to our cemetery.

"I smell purity and incompetence," Wiggles said, his nose in the air.

"You're not the only one." I changed direction, and we headed to the cemetery gates.

Two angels stood outside. Grandpa Lucius blocked their path, his expression stern as he glared up at them.

"Feathers at twelve o'clock," Wiggles muttered. "If either of them tries to hug me like Dazielle did this morning, I need permission to bite."

"Granted. Let's hope it doesn't come to that."

Grandpa Lucius's raised voice drifted toward me, and I increased my pace. "What's going on?"

"Tempest! These angels want to poke around. They don't believe me when I tell them the prison is secure."

I blinked in surprise. I rarely saw Grandpa Lucius angry. He was a laid-back guy, who loved to chill out with a good book and a bit of classical music. Right now, he was anything but chilled. His cheeks burned with color, and his hands were fisted.

"He's right," I said to the backs of the angels. "Stop hassling him."

One of them turned, and I recognized Sablo.

"I'm sure you're right, Tempest. We're here on Dazielle's orders. She's insisting we check for ourselves. We won't be long."

"You're not getting in here," Grandpa Lucius growled. "Whenever an angel steps inside the cemetery, it causes chaos with the demons. They get fixated on breaking out and ripping off your wings. It takes hours to settle them."

"I'm not bothered what the demons think of us," Sablo said. "We have to look around. You might have missed a crack."

I glowered at her as I joined Grandpa Lucius. "We do not miss cracks."

Sablo raised a placating hand. "Demons are tricky. We both know that. We have to take a look."

"Do you think you can do a better job of running this place than we can? We know how to identify any weaknesses and fix them."

Sablo sighed. "Please, we don't want to cause you any problems."

"Then leave," Grandpa Lucius said.

"We can't do that." Sablo glanced at her colleague. It was one of the new, unfriendly angels I'd met this morning. "If you like, you can guide us around. Show us the place is locked down, and we'll leave you alone. We have to make sure Willow Tree Falls is safe. If there's a demon on the loose—"

"If there is, you'll call me to catch it."

Sablo smiled. "We most likely will. Just a quick look that's all I'm asking. We won't touch anything unless you say it's okay to do so."

I raised my eyebrows and looked at Grandpa Lucius.

The muscles in his jaw twitched, but he gave a swift nod. "Okay, so long as you're not wandering around on your own."

"I wouldn't dream of doing such a thing in your cemetery," Sablo said. "Your place, your rules."

"I'll show them around," I said to him. I was worried Grandpa Lucius might lose his temper and shove the angels into the prison. That would be fun for the resident demons.

Grandpa Lucius patted my arm before standing aside. "Don't take any nonsense from them."

That would be tricky. Angels weren't the easiest of magic creatures to deal with. I'd rather deal with a grumpy werewolf or a misbehaving fairy. I walked into the cemetery in front of the angels.

"This is Jophiel." Sablo introduced the unfamiliar angel.

"I take it Dazielle has had a recruitment drive." I nodded at Jophiel.

"The big boss gave us extra funds. We've been having a lot of suspicious deaths lately. We need experts who can deal with the darker side of crime."

Suspicious deaths! I'd helped them to solve most of those suspicious deaths. They should have offered me the job. Not that I'd have accepted. Feathers made my nose itch.

"Don't touch that." Grandpa Lucius hurried up behind us and swatted Jophiel's hand from a sculpture of an angel with her wings extended.

She pouted and looked away. This new recruit needed training.

"I've got this." I winked at Grandpa Lucius. "Wiggles, why don't you keep Grandpa Lucius company?"

Wiggles growled as he glared at the angels. "I wanna come with you."

I knew what he was like around angels. He was longing to take a chunk out of one of these feathered beauties, and I didn't need Dazielle on my back because of Wiggles' bad behavior.

"I've got a breakfast burrito we can share." Grandpa Lucius waggled his eyebrows at Wiggles.

"Burrito beats angels any day." Wiggles bounced around the gravestones. "What are we waiting for?"

Grandpa Lucius eyed the angels with suspicion as he backed away. "We'll be at the family crypt if you need us."

"Thanks, Grandpa."

"How does your demon prison work?" Jophiel asked.

"Much like any other prison designed to contain supernatural nasties. Magic keeps them inside. We monitor them remotely, so we don't have to go in unless there's a problem."

"Do they have cells?"

"No, they're free roaming demons. There are a few who need their own private space, though. They don't do well in company."

"Don't they fight if they're all together?"

"It can get feisty down there, but they figure out their own pecking order. If they don't, they don't tend to survive for long."

"How often do they try to escape?"

"Most days."

Jophiel looked horrified. "You have to fight demons every day?"

"No, a quick whack on the head sorts them out." I grinned at Jophiel. "This way."

I showed them the main entry points to the prison through the Darkmore and Willow family crypts. These were the two oldest families in the village and had established the magic community centuries ago.

Sablo and Jophiel spent a few moments looking around each crypt, running their hands over the cool stone as if their angel fingers could detect something I couldn't.

"It all looks secure," Sablo said.

I nodded. "That's because it is."

"Have you had any problems with cracks opening?"

"Yes. All the time."

Jophiel gasped. "It doesn't sound stable."

"It's very stable. But the ground is old, and the magic gets weak. It's why we always have someone stationed in the cemetery. Usually, we have two people, but with the current situation, Grandpa Lucius is managing on his own."

Sablo looked around the cemetery. "No one got out recently? You would report that to the angels if it happened?"

"Of course. If they had, and we kept the information hidden, our reputation would be in tatters. We don't let demons out once they go inside."

"Which means one of two things."

I nodded. "Either we have a demon on the loose who somehow got into the village..."

"Or, this is much closer to home, and someone you know murdered Bastille."

I hated that that appeared to be the more likely option. "How's the investigation going?"

"We've finished at the crime scene and moved Bastille's body." Sablo swiped her hands down her arms. "It was a horrible way to go."

"Did she fight back?"

Sablo slid me a sideways glance. "Dazielle said you're not to be involved. You know everyone who's a suspect. You're a suspect."

"Which means I'm going to be involved. I know these witches, and I know none of them are killers. I also know I'm not a killer."

Sablo shrugged. "Alibis have yet to be established for everyone."

"I can give you mine now."

"No. This has to be done by the book."

I struggled to conceal my frustration. "It must be someone who lives in Willow Tree Falls. They must have a grudge against Bastille. One they've been holding onto for a long time, just waiting for the right opportunity to get their revenge."

"It's likely to be someone Bastille knows well," Sablo said.

"Which means she didn't fight back!" I jabbed a finger at Sablo. "She knew her killer."

Sablo sighed but nodded. "There was no sign of a struggle. She wasn't dragged into the garden. She went willingly."

"They took her outside the hotel so no one heard any struggle," I said. "They didn't want anyone hearing any noise or stumbling into Bastille's room mid-murder."

"It's looking likely. There are no signs of a fight in Bastille's room or any suggestion she was taken against her will. Bastille went outside alone in the middle of the night with her killer. Her killer was known to her. She trusted them."

I was reluctant to admit that any of Auntie Queenie's friends had anything to do with this, but it sounded like one of them could be involved.

"Could a demon have tricked her?" I suggested as I continued to lead the angels around the cemetery. "A shape shifter. Demons can take human form for a short period. This mystery demon could have disguised itself in order to get to Bastille."

Sablo didn't look convinced. "Why bother? A powerful demon wouldn't have cared if they'd been overheard. Demons are chaos makers. The more damage and death, the better."

"The demon would have been cautious if it realized there were powerful witches in the other rooms."

Sablo tilted her head. "It's possible, but those powerful witches are also on our suspect list."

"If it was a demon, they weren't from here."

"It doesn't look like it." Sablo stopped by the gates of the cemetery. "You run a solid prison."

"I agree." I nodded at Sablo and Jophiel. "Have you started questioning people yet about Bastille's murder?"

"We'll be speaking to everyone," Sablo said, "including you and Queenie."

"I don't want to spoil the surprise, but I'm her alibi and she's mine. After the party, I helped get Auntie Queenie home. Mom was also there. Auntie Queenie was in no condition to harm anyone with magic." Magic needed a clear head to be effective, and that was one thing Auntie Queenie hadn't had last night.

"We still need to check that out," Sablo said. "What about you? How clear was your head?"

"Clear enough, but this has nothing to do with me. What have the other suspects said?" I had to know what progress the angels had made.

Sablo narrowed her eyes. "I'm speaking to Esmeralda and Lila first. We'll get around to Queenie later today."

That gave me an opportunity. If I could get to the hotel and speak to Caprice before the angels did, I could learn how bad the bickering got between her and Bastille. It was a long shot, but my questioning had to start somewhere.

"Is there anything else you need to see?" I smiled sweetly. "Maybe a VIP guided tour in the prison?"

"You're kidding?" Jophiel backed away, her eyes wide.

"Of course she is." Sablo's expression grew pensive. "You are kidding?"

I laughed. "Anytime, you know where we are. The demons will be thrilled to see you."

"We'll report back to Dazielle," Sablo said. "But remember what she said. You need to stay out of this. I've told you too much."

"Don't worry. I always listen to what Dazielle tells me."

Sablo pursed her lips before heading toward the hotel with Jophiel.

I hurried back to the family crypt to find Grandpa Lucius and Wiggles chomping on the last of a giant burrito, alongside a bag of tortilla chips. "They're gone. They found nothing, as we knew they would."

"They're so full of themselves." Grandpa Lucius wiped his fingers on a napkin. "They rile me up with their self-importance. There's nothing like a self-righteous angel to put you off your breakfast."

It didn't look like they'd put him off that much. "Our demons are not to blame for this."

He nodded. "Any substance to the theory of a rogue demon?"

"I hope not, but I need to check it out."

Grandpa Lucius shook his head. "Better that than the other grim option."

"Which is why I can't stop. I need to figure out what happened; otherwise, Auntie Queenie won't get any sleep worrying about who killed Bastille."

"Of course, you go but be careful." Grandpa Lucius stood and kissed my cheek. "There's a killer out there. Whoever it is, demon, witch, or otherwise, they have strong magic."

"I will, but we have to find out what happened." I waved goodbye as I dashed out of the cemetery with Wiggles.

"Good burrito?" I asked him.

"It could have used more hot sauce, but I'm not complaining. A burrito's a burrito. You can never have a bad one."

"Are you ready to sneak past some angels?"

"Of course. It's something I'm getting top marks in lately."

I grinned at him as we dashed to the hotel. I wasn't all that comfortable having to question people I'd known all my life about a murder, but there was no other option.

Sablo wasn't a bad angel, but she wasn't the most competent. I needed to get as much information as I could to piece this mystery together.

And I had to do it before Dazielle figured out what I was doing and followed through on her threat to shove me in a cell until this investigation was over.

62

Chapter 6

As I entered the hotel, I heard voices coming from upstairs, but there was no one on the reception desk.

I snuck a look at the guest book and saw Caprice's room number before hustling up the stairs with Wiggles.

I knocked quietly on Caprice's door.

She opened it a few seconds later. "Tempest! What are you doing here? I thought we were all being kept apart by those irksome angels."

"We are. I'm not supposed to be here." I hurried into the room and shut the door, not wanting any angels to discover me interviewing suspects.

Wiggles jumped on the bed and bounced up and down a few times. "This mattress is too soft."

Caprice scooped him off and placed him on the ground. "Then it's a good job it's not your bed, you bad boy."

Wiggles' tongue flopped out and his tail wagged. "I love a bossy witch."

Caprice shook her head before her attention shifted to me. "How's Queenie doing? We're all so shocked about what happened."

"Like you, she can't believe what's going on. The angels are talking to everyone, but I wanted to get your take on things. Did you see anything unusual last night? Have you got any idea who'd want to do this to Bastille?"

Caprice gestured to a seat in the room before perching on the end of her bed. "Nothing that would be bad enough to kill her."

My eyebrows shot up. "But she was having problems with someone?"

Caprice rested her elbows on her knees. "Bastille lived a basic life. She never had much, not even when growing up."

"Unlike you." I noticed the royal blue outfit Caprice had on was tailored, and a pair of fancy studded designer boots sat by the closet. "I've heard you bickering at previous reunions."

Caprice sighed. "I did tease Bastille when she turned up in second-hand clothes or a dress she'd worn the last time we met. I didn't mean anything by it, but I know it riled her. She was happy enough to call me a snob and stuck up when she was of a mind to. That's how we were."

"Did she have financial problems? Is that why she lived so simply, because she didn't have money?"

"Bastille always said she had enough, but I think she would have liked more. She never complained about being poor, but she'd run into problems recently because of a medical bill she couldn't pay."

"I didn't know she was sick."

"She'd had a persistent cough, but we didn't think it was serious. The trouble is, we only see each other once a year. I couldn't tell you if a cough she had five years ago was the one she had last year. I figured it was an age thing. There's only so much magic can do to stave off the inevitable." Caprice smoothed her hands over her sleek hair.

"Bastille must have worried about this medical bill. Do you know how she planned to pay for it?"

"Oh, yes. Samantha loaned her the money. It wasn't a secret. She has more money than I do. Samantha married well, you see. It's not family money, like mine. Her husband is generous, and she got the money off him to give to Bastille. She didn't want her to worry about an unpaid debt. It could have made her health worse."

"Do you know how much Samantha loaned her?"

"It wasn't discussed. I overheard Bastille thank Samantha and promise to pay it back as soon as she could. Although, how she planned to do that I can't imagine. Bastille had no money. She scraped by on thin air. Samantha wasn't seeing that money back anytime soon, if ever."

That was a possible motive. If Bastille had reneged on that promise and Samantha was in need of her money, it would give her a reason for confronting

Bastille. They could have argued, especially if Bastille had told Samantha there was no money and she couldn't repay her.

I didn't know Samantha's husband, but maybe he was the one pressuring to get his cash back, and Samantha panicked. How would Samantha feel knowing she'd never see the money again? I needed to speak with her next and find out.

"I hope the angels sort this mess out soon," Caprice said. "I wasn't as close to Bastille as the others, but I'd never wish her harm. She was one of us, no matter where she bought her clothes."

"Is there anyone else who might have had a problem with Bastille?"

Caprice played with the hem of her skirt. "I shouldn't say."

"The angels will ask you the same thing." I leaned forward. "What do you know?"

She glanced at me and looked away. "Tempest, I hate to say this, but Bastille and Queenie did argue yesterday at the party."

I jerked back in surprise. I hadn't expected Caprice to point the finger at Auntie Queenie. "I was there. It wasn't a full-blown argument. It was the same thing they always bicker about."

"Exactly, your Uncle Kenny." Caprice smoothed her silk skirt over her knees. "Bastille knew how to hold a grudge. She'd never forgiven Queenie for what happened."

"Auntie Queenie had no reason to kill Bastille. She got her man."

Caprice arched an eyebrow. "Bastille swallowed her pride and her dislike of Queenie, so she could remain a part of the group. She's always civil to Queenie but nothing more. I think, deep down, there was a lot of anger still simmering."

I blew out a breath. "I had no idea. I mean, I knew they weren't that close." Could this be true, and Bastille had been silently seething all these years every time she saw Auntie Queenie?

"Their argument was never resolved. Queenie apologized plenty of times, and Bastille pretended to accept and say it was fine, but she wasn't fine. She held in all her anger. I believe that's part of the reason she suffered such poor health. You bottle your rage and hurt, and it festers like a wound."

"Did Bastille ever talk to you about how she felt?"

"She shut the door on that conversation. I tried several times to get her to open up and say how hurt she was and admit that she still loved Kenny, but she wasn't interested."

I shook my head. "Even so, I know for a fact that Auntie Queenie isn't involved. I was with her last night. I helped get her back home. And I watched her go up the stairs with Uncle Kenny. That was the end of her night. Even if she'd wanted to, she was in no fit state to sneak to the hotel, convince Bastille to go outside with her, and kill her. Her magic wouldn't have been effective. She'd had too much to drink."

Caprice shrugged. "I hope you're right. I'm only telling you what I know. And I'll have to tell the angels what I think."

My eyes narrowed. "Don't drop Auntie Queenie in this. She didn't kill Bastille."

Caprice lifted her chin. "Somebody did. We're all under suspicion."

"What will you tell the angels about your whereabouts last night?" Caprice could be deflecting attention by suggesting Auntie Queenie was involved in Bastille's murder.

"I was here. After the party, I came straight back with the others and went to sleep. I'm not used to these late nights. I fell into bed and didn't wake until Samantha knocked on my door this morning. I'm a sound sleeper. I didn't budge from this bed once I was in it."

That wasn't a great alibi, but I could check with Tabitha, the hotel owner, to see if she'd seen Caprice on the prowl when she was supposed to be asleep. "I've seen you do fire magic."

She pursed her lips. "Yes, I can perform proficiently in all elemental magic, fire magic included. But before you go jumping to conclusions that means nothing, I'd never hurt Bastille."

She might not have hurt Bastille, but she had the power to kill with fire. Caprice also had a lousy alibi. It made me queasy to think she was involved or that any of the wonderful witches I'd gotten to know over the years could be Bastille's killer.

I sighed and slumped in my seat. "I have to figure this out."

"The angels will work out what happened." Caprice patted my knee.

"You have heard about Angel Force?"

"Oh, I know all about them. More beauty than brains. But someone must know what happened to Bastille. Is there any more evidence about a demon being involved?"

"Nothing so far. Our prison is secure and all inmates accounted for. I'm planning a search of the village to be certain we don't have any unwanted guests."

Caprice nodded. "With your help, the killer will be revealed."

"I shouldn't really be helping," I said. "Don't mention that I've been to see you to anyone. I've been told to steer clear of this investigation because I know most of the suspects."

"And you must be a suspect yourself," Caprice said. "Bastille was around when you were growing up, and you were there last night."

"Thanks for pointing the finger at me."

Caprice tutted. "Tempest Crypt, you've just interrogated me and checked my alibi. I get to do the same back. It doesn't feel great, does it?"

She was right. It felt lousy trying to find motives for any of these witches.

I stood and headed to the door. "I didn't mean to offend you, but I have to help Auntie Queenie, and all of you, get to the bottom of this."

"I know. I don't take it personally. We all want to find out what happened." Caprice stood and walked to the door. "I won't say a word to the angels about your sneaky visit. I hope you can solve this."

"So do I. Come on, Wiggles." I opened the door and poked my head out. The corridor was clear of angels.

Wiggles wriggled out from under the bed and joined me in the corridor.

"Which room is Samantha in?" I asked Caprice.

"She's next to me." Caprice gestured to the left.

"Thanks." I whispered a goodbye to her as she closed the door.

"What's our next move?" Wiggles asked.

"Let's see if Samantha's around." I was interested to learn how worried she was that she might never see the money she loaned Bastille. Was she worried enough to kill over it?

Chapter 7

I crept along the corridor with Wiggles and tapped lightly on Samantha's door.

I was pushing my luck. Although I couldn't see any angels, I sensed them, and they weren't far behind me in interviewing Samantha. I had to make this quick.

Samantha opened the door, her green eyes widening when she saw me. "Tempest! This is a surprise."

"I'm on a mission. Mind if I come in?"

"Of course not." Samantha stood to one side.

I hurried into the room with Wiggles and waited as she closed the door. "I'm trying to figure out what happened to Bastille."

"Aren't we all," Samantha said. "Queenie mentioned you've been solving crimes with the angels. What's your theory about this one?"

"I don't have anything concrete. I'm certain none of you did it, although Auntie Queenie mentioned that

Caprice and Bastille didn't get along." I paced the room as I talked.

Samantha cocked her head. "They had their moments. Caprice can be a little full of herself. She even snipes at me."

I stopped pacing. "About what?"

Samantha smirked. "I married well, and she doesn't like that. I've always put her little digs down to jealousy."

"Was she jealous of Bastille?"

"No, Caprice is old money. That comes with an unhealthy dollop of looking down on others. Bastille was never fussed about material possessions or owning a fancy house. If anything, she took pleasure in annoying Caprice by wearing the same outfits when we met. I bet she kept a record of what she wore so she could don it again just to rile Caprice." Samantha chuckled and shook her head. "Bastille had an odd sense of humor."

"Did their arguing ever get intense?"

"Now and again, but Bastille was generally relaxed about it. She took a lot of criticism from Caprice and rarely fired back. Caprice picked on her, but we always warned her off if she got her claws out. Bastille was one of us. It didn't matter how much money she had or if she patched her clothes rather than buying new."

I raised my eyebrows. "Talking of money, Caprice mentioned you gave Bastille a loan."

Samantha pursed her lips. "She does love to gossip. I made no secret of it. As I said, I married well, and a former partner still treats me from time to time, so I always have money to spare."

"Lucky you." Samantha was the youngest of the group at a sexy, redheaded fifty-five, although she looked at least ten years younger. Although she had fine lines around her eyes, they sparkled with vitality, and her curves still attracted the attention of plenty of guys.

"I treat my men well, and they return the favor. Even when we're no longer together." Samantha smiled slyly. "Anyway, we're getting off the point. The money I loaned Bastille wasn't a problem. I said I'd give it to her, but Bastille insisted she pay me back."

"And did she?"

"She paid back a little when she could. She suggested a regular payment plan, but I didn't want to stress her about monthly payments. With her illness concerning her, she had enough going on. If I never saw that money again, it wouldn't bother me. I don't miss it. I don't need it. She did."

"You mentioned Bastille was unwell. Did she use the money for her treatment?"

"Bastille has been unwell on and off for at least ten years. She had periods when she seemed fine, then six months later, she'd be coughing and looking exhausted. Recently, her skin has had a worrying gray tinge to it. There were times when she was so drained she could barely get out of bed."

"No one could figure out what made her so sick?"

"She had all kinds of tests and tried various spells. Nothing stuck for long. The healing and magic treated the symptoms but not the reason for the lingering illness. Every time her illness returned, she seemed weaker. I was worried about her. It's why I was happy to give her money for more treatment, even though it didn't have much effect. She was fine for about eight weeks, but the symptoms crept back."

A worrying thought entered my head. "Could her ill health be related to her death?"

Samantha's eyes widened. "I can't see why it would be. What are you thinking?"

"How desperate was Bastille to get well?"

"I imagine she'd do just about anything to feel better."

"Including making a deal with a demon?"

Samantha's hand went to her mouth. "No! She wouldn't do that. Bastille would never trust a demon. We've dealt with enough of them over the years."

I tapped my fingers against my arm. "If not a demon, could she have tried to heal herself using obscure magic, and it backfired?"

Samantha lowered her hand, concern in her eyes. "Bastille was the weakest of the group when it came to magic, but she still held her own. The elemental essences were never a problem for her, and fire magic was something she managed with ease."

"Did you see her body? Could this have been an accident? A spell went badly wrong, and she injured herself."

Samantha looked away. "I did see her. Unless she choked herself with her own flaming hands, this was no accident."

I sighed. It had been a long shot. "What will you tell the angels when they ask where you were last night?"

"You mean, what's my alibi?"

I shrugged. "I have to ask."

Samantha crossed her arms over her chest. "I was in the hotel."

"All night?"

"I came back with the others."

"You didn't leave your room at any time?"

Samantha bit her bottom lip. "Does it matter if I did?"

"It will if you went into the garden at the same time as Bastille."

Samantha sighed. "No, I didn't do that, but I don't want anybody to know where I was. The girls will tease me."

"About what?"

She teased a strand of hair around her fingers. "I didn't see any harm in it."

I stepped closer. "What did you do?"

"I snuck out for a couple of hours to see my ex. He lives in Willow Tree Falls. It was nothing underhanded, but I didn't want it getting back to my husband. He can be terribly jealous if he sees me so much as talking to another man. I love him dearly and would never be unfaithful, but he has trust issues."

"Okay, so what time did you leave the hotel to see this ex-boyfriend?"

"After midnight, after I was sure everyone was in their rooms. My ex is good to me. He still sends me gifts and checks up on me now and again. It would have been rude if I'd come all this way and not dropped by to say hello."

It did seem suspicious that she just happened to drop by in the middle of the night. Why not meet for coffee in broad daylight when everyone could see what they were up to? I decided not to mention that. "You were catching up for old time's sake?"

"Exactly! There was nothing dubious about it."

"Who's your ex?"

Samantha tilted her head. "Toby Matlock."

I grabbed the wall, feeling certain the room had just tilted. "You used to date Toby?"

She nodded. "We were together for five years."

"I had no idea. What happened to make you separate?"

"Toby's a lovely man and always generous, but he has old-fashioned values. He didn't like me working or traveling without him. He wants a traditional housewife, the kind who'll cook his meals and run around in a frilly apron, fluffing cushions and making sure his slippers are warmed by the fire. That's not me. I love my freedom. I'm not complaining about the wonderful trips we took together or the way he'd shower me with gifts and compliments, but we weren't right for each other."

"I can see why. I'd find it stifling being checked up on all the time."

"As did I. We discussed it like adults. He was honest and said that was what he wanted, and I didn't. I was sad that we parted, but we left it on friendly terms." Samantha shook her head. "I hate to think that Bastille was fighting for her life as I was swanning off to see an old boyfriend."

"If you don't mind me asking, how old were you when you dated Toby?"

"Oh, well, I was in my late twenties. I was involved with the gang and living in Willow Tree Falls. Why do you ask?"

"Toby's the same age as you?"

"That's right. We grew up together. We've been friends since childhood. He was a charming rogue, even back then."

I did a quick calculation in my head and grimaced. Toby was older than I'd thought. If he was the same age as Samantha, he was old enough to be Aurora's father. What was she doing with him? It wasn't that I didn't understand the allure of an older man, but there was old and then there was decrepit.

Samantha touched my arm. "I suspect you're not asking about Toby because of what happened to Bastille."

I rubbed my forehead. "You're right. Toby's seeing a much younger woman. I don't think she has any idea how old he actually is."

"He's a well-preserved warlock. I'll give him that. He uses magic to give himself a more youthful appearance. He likes to hide how old he really is." Her eyes narrowed a fraction. "I had no idea he was seeing anybody. He didn't mention it when we had drinks together."

"They're keeping their relationship quiet, but it's moving fast, and I'm worried. There's talk of them moving in together."

Samantha tossed her hair over her shoulder. "I urge you to tell this young woman to be careful, unless she wants to live the life of a kept housewife, darning Toby's socks and cooking his meals. Toby will expect her to remain at home while he works. He won't like her out, socializing with friends, unless he's there. For all his charm, he's too possessive. Make sure this woman knows what she's letting herself in for."

"I will." I tucked away this information about Toby and Samantha. Despite Aurora being besotted with Toby, I had to tell her what he had in mind for their future. Aurora would never give up Heaven's Door. She'd built a thriving business from scratch. She wouldn't abandon that for a life of tedium as Toby's live-in skivvy and sock darner.

Samantha leaned against the wall and cocked her head. "If you've ruled me out through your not-so-subtle questions, who's next on the list?"

I hadn't completely ruled her out, but her alibi would be easy to check. "Who would you point the finger at?"

"None of us! We all had our squabbles but nothing serious enough to kill over."

"And you didn't see anybody when you went out to meet Toby?" I asked. "You didn't hear voices in the garden or anything like that?"

Samantha twisted her mouth to the side. "I didn't hear voices, but I heard someone walking along the corridor after I got back from drinks with Toby. I poked my head out the door to have a look. I was curious as to who'd be about so late."

I leaned forward. "Who was it?"

"Esmeralda. And she was gone for ages, at least an hour. I was dozing off when I heard her footsteps again and her door close. She's in the room opposite me, so I heard everything."

"Did you see where she went?"

"No, but she went along the corridor."

"Could she have been heading downstairs to the garden?"

Samantha's eyes widened. "Well, it's possible. The stairs are in that direction. But they had no problem with each other. Although…"

"Although what?"

"No, it's nothing. Esmeralda can be sharp with people, but she didn't do that exclusively with Bastille. That's just her manner. She's a no-nonsense sort of woman. She speaks her mind and doesn't care if it offends anybody."

"Has she offended Bastille?" I asked. "Could Bastille have confronted her about something she said and things turned nasty between them?"

"No, that's not Bastille's way." Samantha gave a decisive shake of her head. "The worst she'd do is have a sulk and keep it to herself. Esmeralda's the opposite. She doesn't keep things bottled up. If she wants to do something, she gets on with it. If she discovers a problem, or you've done something to annoy her, you soon know about it because she wants it solved."

I tensed as I heard voices in the corridor. I'd been here too long and had to get out before the angels found me.

Samantha glanced at the door. "I bet those gorgeous angels won't be happy to catch you quizzing me."

I winced when a knock came on Samantha's door. I was out of time. "I need to hide."

Samantha looked around the room. "I'm not sure where to put you."

"Under here's good." Wiggles' voice sounded muffled.

I knelt on the floor and found him under the bed, chewing on what might once have been a pair of Samantha's silky undergarments. "This will have to do." I slid under the bed on my stomach.

"Mrs. Smythe-Barrow," an angel said from outside the room. "We're here about Bastille. Have you got a moment?"

"Are you all set?" she whispered to me.

"I'm good." I tried to yank the remains of the underwear from Wiggles' mouth, but he growled and held on tight.

"I'll be right there," Samantha called to the angels.

I tried to get comfortable under the bed as I heard the door open and Samantha invite the angels in.

Wiggles squirmed over to my side and spat out the soggy fabric. "Not as good as lace," he whispered.

I pressed a finger against my lips as I listened to the angels ask the same questions as I did. Samantha's story was the same. She even admitted to seeing Toby but requested their discretion in confirming her alibi.

My idea that Samantha needed her money back from Bastille had come to nothing as far as finding a decent motive for Bastille's murder. And her alibi would be simple to check, although I wasn't looking forward to having that conversation with the smarmy Toby.

My chat with Caprice also hadn't helped, especially not with her pointing the finger at Auntie Queenie. She was many things, but Auntie Queenie was no killer.

"I'm going to sneeze," Wiggles whispered. His nose wrinkled, and his mouth opened.

I grabbed his mouth and clamped it shut. A flicker of flame drifted out of the corner of his mouth, and the foul stench of brimstone filled the air.

An angel coughed. "Is there something wrong with the plumbing in this hotel?"

"Hmmm, it does smell a little odd in here," Samantha said. "I'll open a window."

I glared at Wiggles, who cocked his ears and wagged his tail.

"It must be the old plumbing pipes," Samantha said. "I've had problems with an unusual smell since I checked in."

"I heard this place is haunted," one of the angels said. "Make sure there's nothing scary under your bed."

I stopped breathing and didn't move, willing the angels not to do anything daft like look under Samantha's bed for things that went bump in the night.

Samantha laughed. "Oh, what nonsense. And, even if there were ghosts here, I'd soon scare them off with a spell or two."

The angels laughed politely.

"Well, if there's nothing else I can do for you."

"No, that's all," an angel said. "We'd appreciate it if you remain in Willow Tree Falls for now, until this matter is cleared up."

"Oh, well, I can't stay too long. My husband's expecting me home." For someone who didn't like possessive guys, Samantha sounded like she'd married badly. Maybe she overlooked his flaws because he had a bulging bank balance.

"This shouldn't take more than a few days. We're confident we'll find who killed your friend."

Samantha let out a sigh. "That's good to know. Let me show you out."

I heard the door open and close.

"It's safe to come out," Samantha whispered.

I crawled out from under the bed, along with Wiggles. "Thanks for hiding me."

"Anytime. You're helping us, so I'm not going to stand in your way." She hugged me. "Oh! Is that where my favorite camisole went?"

I turned to see Wiggles had picked up his new chew toy. "Sorry! He's got a thing for women's underwear."

"You bad doggie." Samantha shook a finger at Wiggles before patting his head. "You'd better keep that. Every time you chew on that, you think of me."

Wiggles wagged his tail, his mouth too full to speak.

"Give my love to Queenie," Samantha said. "I hope to see her later."

"Sure, will do." I hurried to the door and cracked it open. I could hear voices, but I couldn't see anybody.

I said a quiet goodbye to Samantha before we left her room.

I reached the bottom of the stairs without seeing anyone else and had my hand on the door knob when I felt I was being watched.

"Tempest Crypt. Why am I not surprised to find you here?"

Chapter 8

I turned slowly. Dazielle stood behind the reception desk, her arms folded across her chest and a furious gleam in her blue eyes.

I gritted my teeth and tried to smile. "You can't blame me for taking an interest in this case. I knew Bastille. I want to find out what happened."

"Maybe *you* happened to her." Dazielle glowered at me. "Have you returned to the scene of the crime to conceal evidence?"

By the goddess, she was daft sometimes. "You've caught me. Come and watch me as I wrap my flaming hands around another innocent person's neck."

Her nostrils flared. "You know how Bastille died?"

"Of course! Wiggles told me. Remember, you tossed him out of the crime scene."

She scowled at Wiggles. "How could I forget? I still have the faint, unpleasant tang of hellhound on my feathers."

"People would pay good money to smell like me," Wiggles said.

As much as I loved Wiggles, I doubted that. Hellhounds came with a whiff of brimstone and sulfur.

"Tempest, you can't be here." Dazielle rested her hands on the reception desk. "You're getting in the way and only making things harder."

"Until now, no one knew I was here. I've not stopped the angels from questioning people. Have you seen Sablo? I couldn't have been more helpful showing her and Jophiel around the cemetery."

Dazielle nodded. "She did mention that. Who have you been talking to?"

I tried to look as innocent as possible. "What makes you think I've been talking to anybody?"

Dazielle arched an eyebrow. "I'll arrest you for obstructing this investigation if you don't watch your step."

"I've done nothing wrong. I simply had a chat with a couple of Auntie Queenie's friends."

"Which ones?"

I was worried steam might blast out of Dazielle's ears, she looked so angry. "Caprice and Samantha. I wanted to make sure they were okay."

"Sure you did. And while you were doing that, you didn't ask them where they were last night and what their alibis were? And you didn't ask them if they had any problems with Bastille or why they think she was killed?"

I shrugged. "I might have asked some of those questions. They could also have volunteered that information so we can find out who killed their friend."

"Tempest! This is serious. You know everyone involved in this murder. Queenie is a suspect in this murder. So are you."

"No, she's not and neither am I. And the others are as shocked as Auntie Queenie. None of them killed Bastille."

"We won't know that for certain until we've questioned them all."

"Dazielle, you know these witches. They come to Willow Tree Falls every year."

She sighed. "I'll admit it doesn't sit well thinking one of them did this. And we're still pursuing the demon theory in the hope of finding an intruder."

"Yes! Pursue that. That's a great idea." If the angels focused on the demon theory, it would give me more time to question everyone and see if any of the alibis didn't tally.

"No! You pursue it."

My eyes widened. "Me! I thought you wanted me to leave this investigation alone."

"I insist you leave the suspects in this hotel alone. But you're the demon hunting expert. Focus on that. See if we have an intruder in the village."

"I could do with a walk," Wiggle said. "We can have a poke around for a demon while we're out."

Dazielle hissed air through her teeth. "You need your complete attention on this demon hunt. No picnics and gentle strolls. Turn over rocks, look in caves, go to the swamp."

I wrinkled my nose. "You don't know your demons very well. They don't like any of those places. If we had a pole dancing club in the village, that would be my first stop. Then the takeout places."

"We should go to Mystic Mushroom." Wiggles nudged me with his nose. "Pizza! Pizza! Pizza!"

"Not pizza, demon! Focus on the demon." Dazielle shook her head. "I don't know why you keep him around."

"Because his presence makes you so happy." I looked at Wiggles and winked.

Wiggles scratched his belly with a back paw. "Always happy to make an angel's day."

"You won't think I'm interfering if I hunt for the elusive demon?" I had planned on scouting about for a demon but had hoped to speak to all of Bastille's friends before that.

"You being here and ensuring our killer has her story straight is interfering. Demon hunting isn't."

"I didn't do that. I want to find out who killed Bastille as much as you do. I'm not here to cause problems. I'm helping."

"Help by staying out of this hotel." Dazielle walked around the reception desk and towered over me. "You're tampering with witnesses."

"I'm not tampering."

Dazielle shook her head, and the hardness left her eyes. "I know this is personal. It must be difficult for you because you knew Bastille. We will find out who killed her. This case is my top priority."

I blinked back tears at Dazielle's unexpected kindness. "Make sure you do."

"I ask just one thing of you. Leave this investigation alone. We don't need your help. I'll drop by the house to see Queenie later and take her statement."

"You don't want to see her at your headquarters?"

"I don't want to make anything official. Not until we have more evidence."

"So, you do have some evidence? Who have you talked to? What leads do you have?"

Her gaze hardened. "Don't push your luck, Tempest. If you hadn't helped us on previous cases, I'd be sending you to the cells. You wouldn't get released until we figured this out. If I find out that anyone you've talked to this morning has changed her story, I might still do that."

"They won't change anything. They all want to find out what happened. I'm trying to speed things up."

"We're going fast enough. Now, get out of here and don't come back." Dazielle took a menacing step toward me. "This is your only warning. If I catch you snooping around again, you'll find yourself in a cell for interfering in official Angel Force business."

I grumbled under my breath, but Dazielle was right. I was too close to this investigation and struggling to see anyone as the killer. Maybe letting an impartial mind take the lead was the best thing to do. It was just a shame it would be the mind of an angel.

I sent out a silent wish that they wouldn't mess up this investigation.

"Is there something you want to say?" Dazielle tilted her head. "There's nothing you want to confess while you're here?"

I smiled sweetly at her. "Not this time."

"Then go find me a demon, and we can put this case to bed."

I saluted her. "Come on, Wiggles. Let's see what we can find lurking in Willow Tree Falls."

Chapter 9

I dashed to Cloven Hoof, collected my demon catching bag, a pouch of salt, and changed into a pair of boots I didn't mind getting muddy.

"Where are we hunting first?" Wiggles asked. "Please say Mystic Mushroom."

"If there's a demon around, it won't be in plain sight."

"So, behind Mystic Mushroom?"

"You really want pizza at this time of day?"

"Any time of day is pizza time." Wiggles bounced around me. "A quick check of the trash and we can move on."

"You mean, a thorough investigation of the alley behind the store to make sure there's no evidence of a demon trying to get its greedy claws on leftovers."

"That too." Wiggles' eyes glowed. "But if there is a demon, it had better not have eaten all the leftovers."

"I'm sure there will be plenty of garbage for you to sort through."

"Even so, we should hurry." Wiggles dashed down the stairs and barged open the front door.

It was amazing how motivated he got at the prospect of day old pizza. I wasn't so different, but I drew the line at eating pizza from the trash, even though it was made by Tate.

I strode after Wiggles to the alley behind Mystic Mushroom. My gaze swept the area, but there were no clues that screamed demon to me. The large trash container was locked with nothing stacked around it.

"Nooooooo!" Wiggles pawed at the locked container. "Tate's put a lock on it. Why do something so cruel?"

"Because someone was stealing the leftovers." I grinned at him. "Tate doesn't want to attract vermin."

"Hey! I'm not vermin. I'm offering a free clean-up service."

As Wiggles hunted for a way to get the food, I walked along the alley. It was clean, no smell of demon, no goo, no mess. If there was a demon in the village, it hadn't discovered the delights of Tate's pizza.

"We should try the forest. There are plenty of places to hide and wait until after dark before coming out to cause more problems." That was if we were talking your average, annoying demon. Anything stronger wouldn't bother hiding. It would rampage and maim and do whatever it liked.

Wiggles grunted as he kicked the locked trash bin. "How long will we be hunting?"

"It shouldn't take more than a couple of hours to cover the forest," I said.

"Two hours! Then we'll need snacks."

"No snacks. We can have lunch when we're done."

"How am I supposed to concentrate if I'm hungry?" Wiggles eyed the trash container. "I was relying on this hidden feast to get me through this search."

"You can manage for two hours without food."

Wiggles flopped onto his belly. "No! Go without me. I'm too weak to move."

I shook my head. I didn't have time to argue with my greedy hellhound. "Fine. We'll grab something to eat on the go."

He raised his head. "Sweet or savory?"

"You choose. Just make it snappy."

Wiggles hopped to his feet. "Sweet. I've gone right off pizza."

I stopped at Sprinkles bakery and grabbed two cherry bakewell slices.

"Hey, Tempest. I heard from my customers about what's going on at the hotel," Patti Kayes said as she bagged my treats. "How's everybody doing?"

"Not great," I said. "We're still trying to figure out what went down."

Patti's gaze went to the demon bag clipped to my belt loop. "There's truth in the rumor about a demon having done this?"

"It's possible. So far, there's not much evidence to go on." I leaned closer. "The angels don't want me to interfere, but the least I can do is make sure we're safe until they find the killer."

"Absolutely. The last thing we want is another demon causing trouble." Patti winced. "How's Frank?"

I grinned. "Being his usual charming self. This has nothing to do with him, and I'm not even convinced this is demon related. If I can squash the demon rumor, I can focus on finding out who did it. Or rather, the angels can, because I'm not getting involved."

Patti smiled. "I have a feeling you won't leave this one alone."

"I don't know. Being threatened with a few days in a cell has made me hesitant, but I can't sit back while Auntie Queenie is so worried."

"Of course not! I'd be the same. I'll keep an eye out for anything suspicious."

"Like a marauding demon running past the store?"

Patti chuckled. "You'll be the first to know if I spot one of those. Good luck hunting."

"Thanks." I headed out of Sprinkles and walked along with Wiggles as we munched our cherry bakewell slices. The shortcrust pastry was baked to perfection, and the layers of jam and frangipane, topped with flaky almonds, cheered me up.

If there was a demon in Willow Tree Falls, I could deal with him.

I licked the last flakes of pastry from my fingers and focused on the task in hand as we reached the edge of the forest.

The trees absorbed the faint sounds from the street as I walked along a path. This place felt too peaceful to be hiding a demon, but there were all sorts of interesting things lurking in the trees. Fairies, sprites, pixies. There was even the occasional retired werewolf.

Wiggles sniffed the air and lifted one paw. "There's something odd in here. I recognize the smell."

"What are you picking up?"

"There's a hint of demon, but I don't think it's the one we're after. It's not strong, and the smell has faded. It's like he passed through a few days ago and left behind a stink."

"We need a fresh scent trail," I said.

We walked for a few minutes before I slowed. There was a small puddle of dried green goo on the ground. I knelt and touched it gingerly with my finger.

Wiggles peered at the goo. "That looks like a demon excretion."

I studied the goo before wiping my finger on a leaf. "It's not recent. This is congealed. Let's go farther into the forest. I'll use a drawing spell. If there's something in here, the magic will attract them."

We walked for another ten minutes until we found a small clearing among the trees. I pulled out my salt pouch and spread a circle around me. "Are you getting in?"

Wiggles' butt was poking out from behind a tree stump. "No, I'm going for a sniff around. There might be a rabbit close by."

"We're not hunting rabbits. We're after demons."

"I'll look out for any of those as well."

"You're outside the circle of protection," I said. "You'll only have yourself to blame if a demon comes after you."

"Nah! Demons love me. I'll have no trouble if any are around."

"I might," I muttered as I watched Wiggles saunter off through the trees.

I took a few deep breaths and calmed my mind before reciting the drawing spell. It was a basic spell and could be adapted to draw different magic using creatures to you. I was interested in any dark energy in the forest. Where there was dark power, there were often demons.

While I was inside the salt circle, whoever I attracted couldn't harm me. I often used this spell outside of Willow Tree Falls to attract demons. There was something about the magic they could never resist. It was like offering candy to a child with a sweet tooth. They always took the bait.

I finished the drawing spell and waited. If the demon was on the other side of the forest, it would take them a few moments to get to me.

A stillness descended as the birds stopped singing. It was as if they'd sensed something was coming and didn't want to draw its attention.

I turned slowly inside the circle, trying to catch a glimpse of whatever had stopped the birds from making a noise.

A blur of movement caught my eye, and I ducked as an arrow flew at my temple.

"What the—" I dived to the ground as several more arrows shot through the air, aimed straight at my heart. I landed in the dirt and flung a barrier spell over me.

What was going on? I'd never met a demon who shot arrows. They attacked with flames, fangs, and claws, rarely weapons.

I rolled onto my side and peered through the trees. There was no one there, but someone had to be in charge of those arrows.

I moved to a crouch, remaining inside the salt circle. "Show yourself, demon. What business do you have in Willow Tree Falls?"

There was no response and no more arrows. I stood slowly, being sure to keep the barrier spell covering me. I recited the drawing spell once more. Maybe the demon was shy and needed a little encouragement.

The spell prompted no response, and my immediate concern was to discover who was trying to finish me off with arrows. Demon or not, they were in trouble.

As I stepped out of the salt circle, I paused and cocked my head, listening for any sign someone was making their escape. There was nothing other than the faint stirring of dried leaves on the ground.

I headed cautiously in the direction the arrows had come from and walked past several trees, peering around each one slowly to see if my attacker was hiding. There was no one to be found. The forest was quiet, and my attacker was gone.

I returned to the clearing and looked around. The arrows were still there, embedded in the trunk of a tree.

Retracing my steps, I peered among the branches over my head. My eyes widened, and my mouth fell open. Hovering in the air was a bow with an arrow notched in it.

I glanced around, but no one seemed to have ownership of this hovering bow. "It looks like we have a mystical Robin Hood in our woods," I muttered to myself.

This wasn't the work of a demon but a strong magic user. This could be protection magic. Someone had placed the bow here to ward off people and stop them finding something precious that had been hidden. An arrow in the gut would definitely do that.

After another quick scout around to convince myself I was alone, I continued my hunt for the demon.

I paused and sucked in a deep breath. There it was, the smell I'd been looking for. It was the faint, unpleasant stench of sulfur.

"Wiggles, is that you?" I might be picking up on his smell. On a bad day, Wiggles carried the aroma of demon with him.

There was no response from Wiggles.

I moved cautiously through the forest, unclipping my demon bag from my belt. If I was about to be jumped by a demon with flaming hands, I needed to make sure I captured him on the first attempt. There was no way I'd end up like Bastille.

I spotted more green goo on the ground. This looked fresher, and another large blob sat on top of a rock. I hurried over and touched it. The demon had been here recently.

And, if they were leaving fresh blobs of demon goo as they moved, they must be injured. Demons didn't bleed the same way as anyone else. They oozed a sludge-like substance from their veins. Sometimes, it burned if you got any on your skin. Mostly, it just stank.

I kept my attention on the ground as I looked for more goo. If I followed the goo trail, I'd find the demon. And if I found the demon, I'd find Bastille's killer.

I gasped as a web of sticky netting enveloped me. I twisted, feeling the invisible webbing clutch me and dig into my skin. I sucked in a breath, and the webbing slid into my mouth and down my throat, choking me.

Twisting and straining, my heart raced as I struggled to breathe. I needed to get free, but the webbing held fast. This was not demon power enveloping me.

I tried a freeze spell, turning my palms and blasting the spell against the magic that trapped me. The webbing held fast.

My panicked brain went into overdrive. If some enormous, creepy spider with poisonous fangs came to eat me, I would not be happy.

Frank's power curled up my spine as he sensed the danger, but he seemed in no hurry to offer assistance. "It seems you're having a little trouble."

"Nice of you to notice." I spoke to him inside my head.

"You're tied up."

"Again, well spotted. What is this stuff?"

"It has the tang of binding magic. You might like to hurry. It's set to explode."

My eyes bugged. No way was I going to die thanks to gross, sticky, exploding webbing. That would look great on my gravestone. *Here lies Tempest Crypt, renowned demon hunter. Killed by sticky webbing. What a loser.*

The webbing around me grew warm as the magic strengthened.

"You want fire, I'll give you fire!" I blasted a jet of flames from my hands.

The webbing ignited around me and flamed into the sky, singeing my hair as it did so.

My spell worked. The binding magic broke, and I was free to move.

"Congratulations, witch. You live to fight another day." Frank's energy ebbed down my spine as his voice faded.

I snorted in response as I pulled strands of webbing out of my mouth. He must have surfaced because he was worried his free ride was about to combust. Selfish demon.

Grimacing, I tried to brush off lank strands of gray webbing that clung to my clothing. What was going on? Someone had booby trapped the forest.

After getting my breath back, I soon spotted more green goo and picked up the trail, keeping one eye on the goo and the other on any more magic traps.

Maybe a demon had crept into Willow Tree Falls without anyone noticing. This might be a case of Bastille being in the wrong place at the wrong time. She stumbled across the demon, and it destroyed her. But that didn't explain why she was outside so late on her own.

I grimaced as my boot landed in a puddle of green goo. Seeing this much goo, it suggested the demon was badly injured. Bastille could have gotten in a few good shots before she was taken down.

I hoped that was true. I hoped she'd fought like a warrior and made this demon regret ever meeting her. Bastille hadn't deserved to die. When I found this demon, I wanted to find it hurting and sorry. It wouldn't bring Bastille back, but it would give me comfort knowing she didn't give up without a fight.

I followed the goo trail for another twenty minutes, drawing ever closer to the swamp in the forest. It wasn't my favorite place. And it wasn't so long ago that I'd rescued Rhett and Axel from unpleasant deaths when they'd been buried near the swamp.

My boots squelched through sticky mud as I continued my hunt for the injured demon.

I tilted my head. The birds had stopped singing again.

I tensed, half expecting more arrows to fly at my head.

An icy wind blasted past me, and a glimmer of movement made me flinch and duck.

The sound of an enraged warrior's scream filled the air, and a foot brushed past my head. "Back you horror. You foul beast. You dare to invade my forest with your twisted magic."

I knew that voice. It was Fallon, the wood nymph who protected the forest. I turned, but before I could speak, two feet slammed into my back, and I hit the ground face first.

"You desecrate this sacred place. You summon demons to harm what is most precious. You risk the safety of my forest to meet your demon lover."

Demon lover? I spat out dirt and tried to roll over, but something sharp jabbed into the base of my spine. I froze.

"I'll teach you not to come into my forest. Let this be a lesson to you."

I sucked in a breath to shout an objection but was engulfed in a wave of foul, sticky green goo. It washed over me like a putrid wave. I could do nothing but close my eyes and pinch my lips shut as I waited for the goo torrent to subside.

Whatever had been jabbing into my back vanished. "Let that be a lesson to you, foul creature."

I moved slowly, flipping onto my back and risking opening one eye a crack. "Fallon? What are you doing?"

There was a second of silence. "You know me, wretched beast?"

"Of course. And you know me." I swiped the worst of the goo off my face and shook it off my hand. "It's Tempest Crypt."

"Oh! Tempest!" Fallon blinked at me and lowered the thin blade she held. "What are you doing summoning demons?"

I pulled myself into a seated position. "I'm not summoning anything. I came here to see if there's a demon loose."

"In my forest?" Fallon shook her head, her dark eyes narrowed. "I'd never allow such a thing."

"What about the green goo I keep finding? It's all over the place. There's a demon in here somewhere."

Fallon laughed. "That was planted by me. Anyone too nosy for their own good gets lured into my traps. You follow the trail of goo to your doom."

"Your traps? The arrows and sticky exploding web?"

"Oh, sure, that was all my doing. Isn't it great?" Fallon tucked the blade into the belt around her moss green pants. "I upgraded the magic. I got sick of everyone coming into the forest and making a mess, causing noise, and stealing what doesn't belong to them. Some people take acorns and rocks. Who wants those? What do you do with stolen rocks?"

I shook my head. "You could have killed me."

"I know!" Fallon grinned. "It's good stuff."

I raised my eyebrows. "I'll say that again. You could have killed me."

"You look okay to me." Fallon tilted her head. "You're alive. Maybe I need more power in my spells."

"No! No more magic." I wiped goo off my pants. "Does Suki know what you're up to? She's not going to be pleased that you've got lethal magic lurking in the forest."

"Suki's too soft on forest visitors. She used to let anyone come in here and mess around. I had to chase out three lots of campers last week. I gave them quite a scare." Fallon chuckled. "They won't be back."

"The forest is for everyone," I said. "You can't scare people away, even though campers can be annoying."

"I'll scare them out if they do daft things like try to summon a demon." Fallon glared at me. "What made you do such a crazy thing?"

I rested my hands on my knees. "It was a drawing spell, not a summoning spell. There's a big difference."

Fallon sniffed. "They're not so different. You were encouraging a foul presence into my forest."

I squinted at Fallon. "You haven't heard about Bastille?"

"If she's not in my forest, I won't have heard about her. What's she done?"

"She's been murdered. Bastille was a friend of my Auntie Queenie. She was killed last night at the hotel. There's a chance a demon's involved. Bastille was choked to death by flaming hands."

"Flaming hands! There'll be no flaming hands in my forest. Think of the damage to the trees." Fallon glared over my shoulder, her dark gaze flicking around as if trying to spot any demon sporting fire magic.

"This is a good place for a demon to hide," I said. "There haven't been reports of anything odd in the village, so I wondered if the demon was here."

"There are no demons in this forest." Fallon jammed her fists on her hips. "I can guarantee it."

"Since you've got this place so tightly bound with magic, a demon wouldn't last five minutes. I barely did."

"You've got that right. Any demon who comes in here will soon regret it."

"And you've had no unusual visitors? No malevolent presence creeping around that might be responsible for what happened to Bastille?"

"Not last night," Fallon said. "You need to look elsewhere for this killer."

I couldn't help but feel disappointed. If there was no demon, it was back to interrogating old friends, women who'd been in my life since I was young.

Fallon stomped to the nearest path. "I can't stand around chatting. You've set off my magic traps. I need to restock the arrows and sort out my webbing."

"Explosive webbing is a bad idea." I struggled to my feet, cold goo sliding down the back of my shirt.

Fallon cocked her head. "How did you break the magic?"

"I used fire."

"Huh! Fire. I'll need to sort that weakness." Fallon walked off, muttering to herself.

I hurried to the path. "Hey, have you seen Wiggles?"

"No, but tell him I've got a saddle made. Whenever he's ready, we can go for a ride." Fallon raised a hand as she vanished into the dense trees.

I shook my head. There was no way Wiggles would let Fallon ride him. The first time they'd met, she thought he was a weird looking pony and tempted him with carrots so she could get on his back. Wiggles had been less than amused.

I scrubbed the worst of the goo off me with a handful of leaves. This mission had failed. There was no demon hiding in Willow Tree Falls, I was covered in goo, and Wiggles had done a disappearing act.

"Wiggles! Where are you?"

I walked around for twenty minutes calling for him, but he didn't come.

I was exhausted, hungry, and frustrated. Wiggles knew his way home. I bet he'd found a rabbit hole or something nasty to eat and was using his selective hearing to focus on his own mission and ignore me.

This called for a time out and something to take my mind off this mess. I needed Mom's home cooking.

Chapter 10

As I entered Mom's house, I heard laughing and talking in the kitchen. I froze when I got to the kitchen doorway. Rhett sat at the table with a plate of sandwiches in front of him.

I glanced at my goo-stained clothing. This was never the look to go for when stumbling into your squeeze. "Hey! What are you doing here?"

Mom turned and smiled at me. "It was your auntie's idea. She said we all needed cheering up after such a horrible morning. She bumped into Rhett when she went out and invited him to lunch."

Rhett looked at me and shrugged, a sheepish look on his face. "I couldn't say no. I know how good your mom's food is."

I swiped ineffectively at the goo on my shirt. "It's good of you to come and cheer everyone up."

He grinned. "I'm always happy to help."

This was so humiliating. Mom and Auntie Queenie always interfered in my relationships.

"Having Rhett here has taken my mind off of Bastille," Auntie Queenie said. "He's such a charming young man. You picked the right one."

Rhett raised his eyebrows at me as I sat at the table. "I was one of several choices?"

"Of course not." Mom placed more sandwiches on the table. "You were always Tempest's first choice."

I wanted to hide. Instead, I grabbed a cheese and pickle sandwich. "I've been looking into what happened to Bastille."

"Excellent. What have you found out?" Auntie Queenie asked.

"I've been in the forest, demon hunting."

"Did you find one?" Auntie Queenie leaned forward. "You smell like you did."

"No such luck. I encountered a wood nymph with an attitude and a liking for deadly magic." I picked a piece of goo off my arm.

"So, no demon?" Auntie Queenie said mournfully.

"I wish I had found one, but Fallon saw no one in the forest. And other than the evidence she planted to lure me into her magic traps, there was nothing to suggest a demon is on the loose."

"And demons have no self-control," Mom said. "If there was a demon here, it would be drawn to people. It wouldn't be able to resist the tempting smells from the café or bakery."

"I have to agree," I said. "I checked at Mystic Mushroom, but there was no sign of a demon. But before I went demon hunting, I talked to Samantha and Caprice."

"What did the girls tell you?" Auntie Queenie asked.

"Nothing conclusive," I said. "Caprice doesn't have an alibi, as such. She was alone in her hotel room all night. She said she didn't leave and went to sleep after the party."

"That's very possible," Auntie Queenie said. "She was never one for late nights."

I glanced at Auntie Queenie. "Caprice did point the finger at you as the killer because you argued with Bastille last night."

"Typical Caprice, she always gets the wrong end of the stick," Auntie Queenie said. "I always argued with Bastille, and we all know why, but it was never a serious argument. It proves nothing."

"She also mentioned that Bastille had borrowed money from Samantha."

"An unpaid debt would be a good reason for murder," Mom said.

"That's what I wondered, but when I asked Samantha about it, she wasn't bothered about having the money back. In fact, she said she'd have given Bastille the money, but she insisted it was a loan."

"Samantha loves to spend her husband's money." Auntie Queenie chuckled. "He looks like a warty toad who eats too much. It's amazing how a heap of cash can make a toad look extremely sexy."

"How much money did Samantha loan Bastille?" Rhett asked.

"I don't know. The money was to pay for a medical bill," I said.

"What's wrong with her?" Rhett asked.

I looked at Auntie Queenie. "Any idea?"

"We've all known she's been ill for a long time, but Bastille never liked to talk about it." Auntie Queenie helped herself to a sandwich from Rhett's plate. "She must have found a new treatment, and that was what the money was for."

I nodded. "Another interesting thing Samantha told me was that Esmeralda left her room late last night. She disappeared for about an hour."

"Who was Esmeralda sneaking off to see?" Auntie Queenie asked.

"Bastille?" I suggested. "It could explain why there was no sign of a struggle. Bastille wouldn't think it odd her friend wanted to see her alone."

"Didn't they get along?" Rhett asked.

"They got along fine," Auntie Queenie said. "There's no reason for Esmeralda to be involved."

I considered mentioning Samantha's late-night rendezvous with Toby, but I wanted to check that out myself. I needed to find out just how friendly Toby still was with Samantha. I could check her alibi without letting everyone else know he was involved.

"If I had to wager, I'd be looking hard at Caprice for this murder," Rhett said. "Her alibi is lousy. What magic ability does she have?"

Auntie Queenie scratched her chin, a doubtful look on her face. "She's an elemental witch, specializing in fire. There are few who can beat her ability to control flame. The heat courses through her like blood. Flame is drawn to her."

"Could Caprice control it so she flamed just her hands?" I asked. "She could have used fire when she choked Bastille to make it look like a demon attack. It's certainly muddied the evidence and our focus. When the angels first discovered Bastille's body, they were drawn to the idea of a demon attack."

"Unless something's happened between them that I don't know about, Caprice wouldn't want Bastille dead," Auntie Queenie said.

"She should be at the top of your suspect list," Mom said. "I like Caprice, but she has no alibi, and she has the ability to kill Bastille with fire, without injuring herself."

"I still need to talk to Lila and Esmeralda," I said. "I want their take on things, see if they heard anything odd last night. I'd have tried when I was at the hotel, but the angels threw me out."

"That won't be a problem," Auntie Queenie said. "I've been in touch with the angels. Once they've interviewed everyone, we're allowed to see each other. They'll be done by the end of the day, and we've got a reservation at Bite Me at seven o'clock. Join us, and you can speak to Esmeralda and Lila then."

"Are you sure the angels don't mind you all meeting?" I could imagine how annoyed Dazielle would have been when Auntie Queenie announced a dinner date with all the murder suspects.

"Even if they do, it won't stop us. It wasn't any of us, so there's no harm in meeting for a good natter over a few glasses of wine and some decent food."

"Then I'll be there." I gazed at my untouched sandwich and sighed.

"What's wrong?" Mom touched my hand. "Are you finding this hard?"

I nodded. "I can't believe it's anyone in this group, which means we've got a killer on the loose in Willow Tree Falls and no idea who it is."

No one spoke for a moment.

Auntie Queenie finished her sandwich and smacked her lips together. "We can't have that. I should get the gang back together. We'll organize a hunt for this killer. No one hurts a member of my gang and gets away with it."

Rhett shifted in his seat. "There's only one gang in Willow Tree Falls, Queenie."

Her eyes narrowed. "And we both know why that is."

They glowered at each other before Mom broke the tension by sliding a plate of warm chocolate chip cookies into the center of the table.

Auntie Queenie grabbed a cookie. "Lovely. My favorite." She broke it in half and dunked it in her coffee.

Rhett relaxed in his seat and took a cookie. "It's not a bad idea to do a search. My guys are available if you need more eyes on this."

"Let's see what information Esmeralda and Lila have first," I said. "We have no clue who or what we're looking for. A stranger? A local gone bad? We'll be searching for someone without knowing who it is we're looking for."

"It makes me sick with worry thinking it might be someone in my gang," Auntie Queenie said. "It must be an outside party. Someone who's taken a disliking to Bastille."

"If anyone can figure this out, Tempest can." Rhett patted Auntie Queenie's hand. "She's good at solving puzzles."

Auntie Queenie smiled at him, all animosity gone. "You're right. She's great. You're lucky to have her."

He smiled at me, and his dark eyes twinkled. "Don't I know it."

I didn't share Auntie Queenie's confidence in resolving this quickly. The only possible, tenuous suspect I had was Caprice, and I hoped I was wrong about her.

I also needed to find out what Esmeralda had gotten up to last night and confirm what Lila did after the party. But if the angels had discovered anything suspicious about them during their questioning, they wouldn't allow the old gang to meet, so I wasn't hopeful of discovering anything useful.

I hoped my questioning tonight would come to nothing, but if it didn't, we might never find who murdered Bastille.

"Thanks for lunch. It was great." Rhett pushed back his chair. "I need to get going."

"Wait a moment." Mom dashed around the kitchen and handed him a tin of cake. "Take this to the gang.

There's plenty more if they want it."

"Thanks, Mrs. Crypt." Rhett grinned. "They'll love this. They don't get a lot of home comforts."

"Please, it's Cora, and they're always welcome to my home comforts."

Auntie Queenie cackled saucily. "Don't tell me you've taken a fancy to a biker?"

"Of course not! What did I say?" Mom looked confused.

"Ignore Auntie Queenie," I said. "She has a dirty mind."

Rhett grinned at my mom. "You're way too good for any of the guys in my gang."

She blushed. "I didn't mean anything by that. I just —"

"Rhett, I'll walk you out." I kissed Mom's cheek as I passed her. I didn't want her getting any more confused about her offer of home comforts to rough, tough biker types.

I accompanied him outside to the garden gate.

Rhett turned and took hold of my hand. "Your mom does a great spread."

"Sorry you got dragged into this."

"I'm always happy to eat good food and make sure Queenie is okay. Despite being a member of a former rival gang, I like her. She's obviously shaken by this murder."

"We all are."

"It looks like you're going to be busy tonight." Rhett glanced back at the house. "Do you really think one of Queenie's friends did this?"

"It's possible," I said. "Bastille proved herself that old wounds fester, and it's not hard to imagine a friendship turning sour. This gathering could be the opportunity her killer was waiting for. Get everyone together, cause confusion, and then attack. Bastille had her guard down. She wouldn't have seen this coming."

"Don't take too many risks finding out who did this." Rhett wrapped an arm around my waist and stepped closer. "You need to watch out you don't get too singed around the edges."

"You mean even more than I already am?"

He touched a strand of my frazzled hair. "You pull off the goo splattered, singed look well."

I smiled up at him, and my heartbeat sped up. "You know I can look after myself."

"And you know that the offer of help is always there if you ever want to take me up on it." He pressed a gentle kiss to my lips. "Any chance our stargazing date tonight is still on?"

I bit my bottom lip and shook my head. "I can't miss this dinner tonight, and I don't know how late I'll be. Everyone will be there. It's my chance to question them and see what theories people have."

"I get it. Family first. I'd expect nothing less from you." Rhett kissed me again.

For a second, I forgot my worries about a killer on the loose in Willow Tree Falls and enjoyed the feel of Rhett's strong, solid arms around me.

"You're going to have to make this up to me," he whispered against my mouth. "You're standing me up."

"If you were a lesser man, you'd hold it against me."

"That's true, but I won't forget. Our next date is going to be epic to make up for this."

I smiled up at him, feeling ridiculously breathless. I was in so deep with this guy, and I couldn't be happier.

Chapter 11

"I shouldn't come tonight." I stood at the front door of Mom's house, peering into the gloomy evening.

"Nonsense! You must. Everyone will be there. You said yourself, you need to speak to Esmeralda and Lila." Mom squeezed my shoulder.

"This is so unlike Wiggles." He hadn't returned from our trip to the forest. It had been seven hours, and he was never away from home for this long. His rumbling belly always enticed him back.

"Wiggles is a robust, clever hellhound." Mom nodded at me. "If he's run into trouble, he can look after himself. After all, he burps flames."

"Only when under pressure."

"There you go. If he has any problems, he can deal with them."

"Oh, wait! I see him." I ran to the gate, relief filtering through me. I hated Wiggles going missing.

A couple of hours wasn't a problem. I was used to that. But anything longer and I got worried.

Wiggles scurried toward me. He was covered in mud, his expression grim. "Where were you when I needed help?"

"What happened?" I stared at him in horror. He was filthy, his paws caked in mud, and his fur grubby.

He wrinkled his nose, his eyes glowing. "I fell in a hole."

"Were you hurt?" I hurried over. "Was it a deep hole?"

He growled at me. "I'm fine. It wasn't deep. I could poke my nose out the top, but the sides were muddy. You know I'm not great at jumping. I bounced up and down a hundred times. I kept flipping on my back. It was humiliating."

I bit my lip. "You've been in a shallow muddy hole this whole time? You really couldn't jump out?"

"Small hellhounds carrying a little extra weight don't have the ability to jump great distances." He turned, displaying how grubby he was. "I stink. I'm cold, and I'm starving. This is all your fault."

"Oh, Wiggles!" Mom hurried to join me. "You poor baby. What happened to you?"

"Ask my negligent owner. She left me in a huge pit. I think there was a snake at the bottom."

"A snake!" Mom gasped.

Wiggles snorted. "Or it could have been a pointy stick that looked like a snake. I was spooked after being abandoned."

"Hey, that's not fair. How was I to know you'd stumbled into a hole and couldn't jump out because of your pot belly? I almost died in the forest, thanks to Fallon. She shot at me, trapped me in magic, and covered me in goo."

Wiggles bared his teeth. "It's no less than you deserve for abandoning a pet."

"I didn't abandon you! I figured you'd gone off hunting a fun scent or found a cute female to hang out with." I was secretly relieved he was back. I'd have to check this hole wasn't another of Fallon's traps to stop people from going into the forest. She took her role of Forest Guardian way too seriously.

Mom fussed around Wiggles. "Come inside, gorgeous boy. I've got a stew almost ready, and you need a bath."

Wiggles expression softened, and he stopped growling. "Can I eat my stew in the bath?"

"No!" I said.

"Of course you can." Mom patted his head. "You've had a stressful day. A big bowl of stew and some of my magic bath salts will see you right."

"I need a belly rub as well," Wiggles said. "I'm very stressed."

"Absolutely." Mom scooped him up and carried him into the house.

He looked at me over Mom's shoulder and stuck out his tongue.

I shook my head. No wonder I had such a spoiled hellhound. Everyone treated him like a prince, me included.

"Come on. Let's go." Auntie Queenie dashed out of the house.

"It's your fault we're running late." Auntie Queenie had changed her outfit three times. She'd gone from a floaty cream number to a scarlet smock and now sported a slightly too tight purple tube dress. I'd opted for a subtler black number that came with a few sparkles.

"We can't keep the girls waiting." She tucked her arm in mine, and we sped along the street toward the restaurant.

I glanced at her. "How are you feeling about this evening?"

"Oh, I'm not worried." She waved a hand around. "I mean, no one has anything to hide."

"That's right. We'll confirm everyone's alibi and spend the evening working out who had it in for Bastille."

"Exactly. You'll solve this, and we'll have no more quizzing from those silly angels."

Although she put on a brave face, Auntie Queenie was nervous. I would be too if my oldest friends had been earmarked by the angels as potential killers.

I pushed open the door to Bite Me and strode in with Auntie Queenie beside me. The scent of vanilla candles, mixed with expensive perfume, filled the air.

"There they are," Esmeralda called as she waved at us.

Lila, Samantha, and Caprice also greeted us as we sat at the table in the corner of the restaurant. The place was busy, with most of the tables occupied. It was no surprise. Tilly Machello always knew how to tempt diners in with her delicious dishes.

"We wondered if the angels had arrested you." Samantha grinned as she poured champagne into our glasses.

"Not likely, but I got a grilling this afternoon, the same as the rest of you," Auntie Queenie said. "They asked me about my relationship with Bastille and any problems we'd had."

"What did they think about you stealing Bastille's man?" Caprice wiggled her eyebrows.

Auntie Queenie squinted at her. "You know that's not what happened. But they kept circling that information like they'd found a perfect motive. I was honest with them about what happened. They also talked to Kenny and left convinced I didn't do it."

"They'd better be convinced," I said. "You've got a great alibi, and you're innocent."

"As we all are." Esmeralda stood from her seat. "This calls for a toast. Bastille was one of the good ones. She didn't have the smoothest ride in life, but she was loyal and honest. Her death was tragic."

"Her murder, you mean," Lila said.

Esmeralda nodded. "I'd like everyone to take a moment to remember a happy memory about Bastille and how she touched our lives." She raised her glass. "To Bastille. One of the best Dead Tree Witches there was."

Everyone raised their glass and toasted to Bastille.

As Esmeralda sat down, Samantha stood. "Since we're commemorating lost gang members, we never got around to remembering our fallen sisters last night."

"Fallen sisters?" I whispered to Auntie Queenie.

Auntie Queenie raised her eyebrows. "Being a gang member isn't plain sailing. It can get rough. People get hurt. People die. Although, this lot didn't die on my watch."

"They've been gone over ten years, but they'll never be forgotten. Let's toast to the memories of Abigail, Petra, Mona, and Kat. They helped make our gang great and are sorely missed."

There was another round of glasses chinking.

"Who were these witches?" I asked Auntie Queenie.

"They were great fun," Auntie Queenie said. "They were in the gang for years. When the four of them turned thirty, they decided to spend a year traveling. They saved up and made a plan of places they wanted to visit."

"They did it all," Caprice said. "They went to Canada and saw polar bears, did a road trip across America and ate greasy giant burgers at all-night diners. They even headed to Mexico and took part in the Día de los Muertos."

"The day of the dead," Auntie Queenie translated. "A public holiday to remember lost loved ones. It's very colorful, and I hear the food served is something else."

"That was around the time they visited the Inca ruins," Lila said, "and where their problems began."

"What problems?" I asked.

"We don't know that the trip to the ruins caused their problems," Caprice said. "But something bad might have gotten them."

"What do you mean by bad?" I asked.

"That's nonsense!" Esmeralda said. "They most likely got bitten by a bug and contracted some exotic disease. I told them to get their shots before they left."

"It wasn't a bug bite that made them unwell," Lila said. "But they were all sick when they came home. The Inca ruin was the last place they visited. When they got back, they had fevers and sore throats and complained of odd visions. I believe there was dark magic in that place. Somehow, it infected them. They were never the same after that trip."

I leaned forward in my seat. "Could they have activated some ancient magic that attacked them?"

"Nobody knows," Auntie Queenie said. "Over the next two years, they faded. They became lethargic and complained of aches and pains."

"It's like the curse in that Egyptian tomb," Lila said. "Tutankhamun's curse. Everyone who went in there when it was first opened became ill. Many of them died or went mad."

"Because of an air borne virus, not a curse," Esmeralda said.

"Many believe Egyptian pharaohs had magic," Lila said. "How else could they build those incredible structures?"

"Slave labor," Esmeralda said.

"Anyway, within two years, our friends were dead," Auntie Queenie said. "It was tragic."

"To our fallen sisters." Samantha raised her glass again. "We'll never forget them."

As the waiter came to take our order, I leaned over to Auntie Queenie. "Their deaths were from natural causes? This bug, or whatever it was, killed them?"

"No, it wasn't the bug, although it definitely weakened their magic. Kat was hexed. Mona had a bike accident. Petra's heart failed, and Abigail died in her sleep."

"All within two years of each other. Isn't that suspicious?"

She peered at me, her forehead wrinkling. "Their doctors noted nothing suspicious. In theory, the hex shouldn't have killed Kat, but she was weakened by this exotic bug. Mona simply lost control of her bike and hit a tree."

I sat back in my seat. "What caused Abigail's heart to fail?"

"The doctor said there was a weakness in a valve. No one noticed it. And Petra had a love of fatty food. She was a touch on the curvy side and was supposed to be watching her calories. One too many pastries caught up with her."

I toyed with my fork. "It seems odd that they died one after the other, even though the causes of death are different."

"It was the Inca ruins," Lila said with a decisive nod. "They messed around with old magic, and it bit back."

I nodded. If no one else considered it strange, it would do me no good to poke around in the deaths of four long-deceased witches. Not when there was a very recent death to focus on.

The waiter left with our order.

I paused with my glass halfway to my mouth as everyone's attention turned to me.

"How's the sleuthing going?" Caprice asked me. "You did a great job questioning me. Better than the angels."

"Yes, what have you learned?" Esmeralda asked.

I lowered my glass. "Nothing that points to a killer, although we can rule out a demon. There's no evidence of one in Willow Tree Falls."

"From what Dazielle said when she interviewed me, the angels have come to the same sticking point," Auntie Queenie said. "They've got no firm evidence. Nothing that points to any of us."

"Which makes sense, because we're all innocent," Caprice said.

"Yet somebody had it in for Bastille," I said. "And they knew her well enough to convince her to go outside with them. They wanted to be alone with her so they could kill her."

Samantha dabbed her eyes with a napkin. "It's so terrible. She was such a gentle soul."

"She was the best," Lila said.

Nobody spoke as hankies were produced and noses dabbed.

Caprice pushed back her chair, her eyes full of tears. "I'll be back in a minute. I need to powder my nose." She stood from the table and walked away.

Esmeralda sighed. "Bastille was lonely. I got the impression she'd given up on life and finding love. She'd shut herself away from everything. She was barely living a life."

"What life she had still deserved to be protected," Auntie Queenie said.

"Bastille was hiding because she was so sick," Lila said. "She kept away from everybody because she didn't want to reveal how bad she was. I knew the truth. She couldn't hide it from me. My senses tingled every time we got close."

I nodded. As a healing witch, Lila had a sixth sense when someone was suffering.

Lila continued. "When I spent time alone with Bastille, I could feel her pain. She put on a good front, but when she thought no one was paying attention, I could sense how awful it was for her."

Esmeralda shook her head. "It wasn't an illness making her distant. If you ask me, dark magic was draining her."

There were several gasps from around the table.

"Bastille didn't use dark magic," Auntie Queenie said.

"That you know of," Esmeralda said. "She wasn't suffering a physical illness, but she was losing herself to the darkness. The signs were there, the pale skin, nervousness, withdrawal from society. She was in trouble."

"That can't be right," Lila said. "I never saw her using anything dark, and I never felt anything toxic from her. Dark magic leaves a residue, no matter how careful you are. It stains you like ink."

"There are cloaking spells that hide dark magic use," I said. It hadn't been so long ago that I'd encountered a member of my own bar staff who'd concealed her use of dark magic under a clever spell. She'd fooled us all.

Lila shrugged. "If Bastille was using dark magic, I don't blame her. She was desperate to find something to make her feel better. Perhaps she turned to the dark arts as a last resort. She felt like she had no other option. She longed to be well, and nothing worked for her."

"Whatever her health problems were, she's at peace now," Esmeralda said.

"If you consider being murdered peaceful," Auntie Queenie said.

Esmeralda's expression tightened. "I meant no longer in pain."

Auntie Queenie sniffed. "She could have asked for help."

"She was proud and fiercely independent," Lila said. "You know that."

Auntie Queenie shuffled her cutlery around on the table. "I do. She never liked to complain."

Lila looked at me. "So, the angels aren't close to charging anyone?"

I glanced toward the restroom. Caprice had yet to return. "Would you be surprised if I suggested Caprice as the killer?"

Nobody spoke for several seconds as they exchanged worried glances.

Esmeralda was the first to speak. "Caprice has power."

"No, I can't believe that," Samantha said. "Caprice is a good witch. She's not a killer."

"If not Caprice, then what about you?" Esmeralda asked.

"What about me?" Samantha stiffened in her seat.

"What's your alibi for the time of Bastille's murder?"

Samantha's gaze shifted to me. "I have an excellent alibi. I've already told Tempest and the angels."

I nodded, deciding not to share her late-night meeting with Toby. That was her secret to tell.

Samantha glared at Esmeralda. "If we're pointing fingers, then what were you doing sneaking out of your room late at night? Going to the garden to see Bastille?"

Esmeralda's jaw dropped. "Absolutely not. I visited Lila. I couldn't sleep and knew Lila stayed up late. I went to her room, and we had cocoa together."

I looked at Lila, and she nodded. "That's right. We sat up chatting for a while. I must admit I was tired and dozed off a couple of times, but that's what happened. We were with each other. After we finished our cocoa, we both went to bed."

There were the alibis I'd been missing. Esmeralda and Lila were together when Bastille was killed.

"What have I missed?" Caprice sat back in her seat and looked around. Her smile faded. "What's wrong?

Don't tell me I have toilet paper stuck to the back of my pants?"

"We were talking about Bastille's murder," Esmeralda said. "Remind us again what your alibi was?"

Caprice blinked rapidly. "You know my alibi. I was asleep. After we finished partying, I returned to my room the same as all of you and went to bed. I didn't stir all night."

"We only have your word for that," Esmeralda said.

"Now, now," Lila said swiftly. "We're not accusing anybody of anything. We're just getting to the bottom of what happened to Bastille."

"You think I had something to do with it?" Caprice leaned back in her seat, a look of horror on her face. "Why would I kill her? We were friends."

"You teased her. You made fun of the fact she had to buy second-hand," Samantha said. "I told you off about that several times, but you still kept on."

"That was our way," Caprice said. "Bastille accused me of being snooty, so I teased her about, well, not having much money."

"Of being poor." Samantha shook her head. "That's not funny. It upset Bastille."

"She never said anything to me about being upset," Caprice said. "If I'd thought I was hurting her feelings, I'd have stopped. I meant nothing by it. I'd always help her out if she ever got into difficulty."

"Bastille would never have asked you for money," Samantha said. "It's why she came to me when she couldn't pay her medical bill. She knew what you'd say to her. You'd tease her about her lack of savings."

Caprice clutched her champagne flute. "Of course I'd have paid her medical bills if she was in debt. None of us wanted to see Bastille struggle financially. But she chose that life. She didn't need to seclude herself and work part-time. It wasn't my fault she was poor."

"It was your fault that you kept prodding her about it," Samantha said.

Caprice glared at her. "Why are you all picking on me?"

"We're not." Lila looked around the group and sighed. "But we're all anxious to find out what happened."

"As am I." Caprice flung her napkin on the table. "I can tell you this right now. I didn't kill Bastille. I loved her the same as any of you. Sure, we bickered, but that doesn't mean I didn't like her. Queenie argued with her much more than I did. Why don't you call the angels in to arrest her?"

Auntie Queenie opened her mouth to argue, but I grabbed her arm and shook my head.

"Everybody take a breath," Lila said. "We're all getting worked up about nothing. We trust each other, and we all have alibis."

"Some of us have better alibis than others," Auntie Queenie muttered.

"We need to look outside our circle for the killer," Lila said.

"It seems you're doing the exact opposite." Caprice stood and shoved her chair back.

"Don't go," Lila said. "We can't fall out about this. We need each other."

"It looks like that's exactly what we need to do." Caprice grabbed her purse and stormed out of the restaurant.

I exchanged a surprised glance with Auntie Queenie.

She shrugged. "We've touched a nerve."

"No, she's just upset." Lila looked at the door as it swung shut behind Caprice. "Although, it is out of character. Caprice is usually so happy-go-lucky."

"Why run if you're not guilty?" Samantha arched an eyebrow and took a sip of champagne.

I looked at Caprice's empty seat.

Samantha was right. Caprice's behavior suggested she had something to hide. It made her look guilty, but how could I prove that?

Chapter 12

I headed to the hotel the next morning with a freshly bathed and sweet-smelling Wiggles to speak to Caprice.

Despite the best efforts of the group, they hadn't been able to get Caprice to return to the restaurant last night. In the end, we'd stayed and eaten, but everyone was mourning the loss of Bastille and not in the mood for fun.

The party had broken up early, with promises to meet the next day and get to the bottom of what happened to Bastille.

I'd been tempted to visit Caprice last night and ask her why she'd stormed off but decided she needed a night to cool down. Everyone showed their grief in different ways, but she shouldn't have reacted so sharply. We were all under the spotlight for Bastille's murder, and Caprice knew she'd have to face questioning, just like the rest of us.

"You're looking handsome today," I said to Wiggles.

"I'm still not talking to you."

I tilted my head, tempted to point out that was exactly what he was doing. "Did you enjoy your stew?"

"Yes."

"And your bath?"

"Yes."

"Do you want to know if I found the killer?"

Wiggles snorted. "If you had, we wouldn't be up so early, marching around before we'd had anything to eat."

It looked like I had some making up to do with my hellhound. "How about a muffin?"

"Make it a tray of muffins, and I might be open to negotiations."

I shook my head as I walked into the hotel reception to find the owner, Tabitha Dimples, behind the desk. Her glasses were perched on the top of her head as she smiled up at me.

"Tempest, how's everything? How's your auntie doing? I bet she's in shock after what happened to her friend."

"She is. We're doing our best to figure out what happened. Actually, that's why I'm here. I was hoping to speak to Caprice. Have you seen her around?"

"I have. She was up early today. She left about an hour ago."

My eyes widened. "Left as in checked out?"

"Oh, no. She said she couldn't sleep and was going for a walk and to get breakfast. She'll be back."

I let out a relieved sigh. For a second, I thought Caprice was making a run for it. "You're sure about that?"

"Absolutely. Her room's been cleaned, and her things are there." Tabitha sucked in a breath. "Why? You don't think she's got anything to do with what happened in my beautiful garden, do you?"

"No. But I have a few questions to ask her."

Tabitha shook her head. "It's a tragedy. All my flowers are dying. I think they're in mourning, too."

"They are?"

Tabitha nodded. "Flowers are sensitive to bad vibes. I'll have to get some cleansing magic from Aurora's store to remove the negativity. And there's nothing like a murder to bring down the reputation of an establishment."

"I'm sure Bastille would agree. She'd much rather be alive and eating a croissant from the buffet than her cold body being pored over by the angels."

"Oh! Of course. That was insensitive." Tabitha pulled her glasses from her head and placed them on her nose. "I'm sad about what happened. I just wish it hadn't been here. I don't want to get a reputation for running a haunted hotel."

"You never know. It could be good for business."

Tabitha peered at me from over the top of her glasses. "Business is just fine as it is."

I repressed a smile. Some people coming to Willow Tree Falls might expect to see a ghost or two. "I'll come back later and see if Caprice has returned."

I tapped my fingers against my arm. I couldn't put it off any longer. It was time to pay a visit to someone who left a bad taste in my mouth. I needed to confirm Samantha's alibi, and that meant a visit to Toby Matlock. I was also interested to see his reaction when I mentioned his relationship with Samantha. I had to make sure he wasn't cheating on my sister.

We left the hotel and walked to the other end of the village, where all the expensive houses were built. It was a short walk, but every step took me closer to luxury I could never afford.

Wiggles wolf-whistled as we approached Toby's house. "Here's a guy who knows how to spend too much money."

I had to agree. Toby's house was an enormous three-story building. There were brick chimneys on either end and a gravel driveway that curved around a lawn large enough to build several more houses on. Giant stone dragons sat atop pillars at the entrance of the driveway.

"I can see why your sister is into this guy," Wiggles said. "He's got more money than sense."

"Aurora's not that kind of woman. If Toby doesn't treat her well, she won't stick around, no matter how loaded he is."

"It happens. Money attracts hot women. And a lot of money makes plain, boring guys handsome. Even a mean guy can be tolerated if he showers you in giant dog bones."

"I get that, but Aurora has her own money. She's a successful business woman."

"She doesn't have this kind of money. Aurora doesn't have giant stone dragons sitting outside her door. And if I'm not mistaken, that car is worth more than everything you own times about a hundred." Wiggles ambled over to a sleek, black car.

I had no clue about cars, but this one looked fancy. Few people drove in Willow Tree Falls. Everything was easy enough to walk to, and magic often interfered with electrical equipment.

"Let's hope Mr. Fancy Pants lets us in, looking like this," Wiggles said. "I should have worn my bow tie."

I resisted the urge to smooth my hair and check if there was mud on my boots. Toby would have to take us as he found us. I knocked on his door, and we waited.

I looked at Wiggles. "Sorry about not helping you out of that hole. I didn't think you were in trouble. I did look for you."

He inspected an urn by the door. "I know. I heard you calling."

"You should have shouted. I'd have found you."

Wiggles wriggled his nose. "I might have found an interesting smell. I didn't want to be distracted."

My eyes widened. "You little sneak. You've made me feel terrible, and all the time, you could have come when I called you. You fell into that hole after I left because your nose led you into a trap."

He glanced up at me. "The hole had a currant bun at the bottom. I couldn't leave that for anyone else to find."

"I thought you said the scary hole had a snake in it."

"There was a sharp stick. In the right light, it looked like a snake."

"So you fell in the hole because you were after food?"

He shuffled his paws. "I might have climbed in and gotten stuck."

I snorted a laugh. "Was the bun worth it?"

"Not really, it was stale." Wiggles nudged me with his nose. "Anyway, apology accepted."

"Apology taken back," I muttered.

A seven-foot butler with a blank expression on his long, pale face opened the door. He peered down at us without speaking.

I cleared my throat. "Hi, there. We're here to see Toby. Is he in?"

"Name?" The zombie-faced butler's voice resonated in his broad chest.

"Tempest Crypt and Wiggles."

"Do you have a meeting?"

"Nope, just passing and wanted to say hi."

He nodded before pushing the door shut in our faces.

"I've never seen him before," Wiggles said. "Do you think he's alive?"

"His skin is weirdly pale. Maybe Toby made him in his creepy lab in the basement."

"Built from the body parts of his victims." Wiggles shuddered.

My eyebrows shot up. "What victims?"

"You know, all the people who've crossed him. I bet Toby doesn't do the killings himself. Maybe his butler does it for him. Toby's built himself a lethal assassin."

I stared at the door, wondering if it would be rude to make a run for it. "I'm sure he's a lovely guy when you get to know him. He's just on the large side."

"The creepy large side. Have you ever read Frankenstein?"

"Have you?"

"I watched the movie. This is Frankenstein's monster, the twenty-first century version."

"Toby is not Doctor Frankenstein." But he was an enigma and one I was determined to get to the bottom of if he continued to date Aurora.

The door opened again, and the butler gestured us inside.

I looked around and failed to prevent my jaw from dropping. We'd stepped inside a palace. The walls were a sumptuous deep red, and my boots sunk into the thick carpet.

"This way." The butler turned and walked ahead of us, his long arms hanging loosely by his sides.

Before I could stop him, Wiggles bounded ahead and walked alongside the butler, looking him up and down. He sniffed his leg and backed away.

I shook my head as I took in the rest of the surroundings. I was no expert, but the oil paintings and vases I passed looked ancient and expensive.

The butler stopped by a door and knocked before pushing it open. He gestured for us to go in.

I poked my head inside. Toby sat behind a large carved oak desk. He was in a library, the walls covered in books, and an enormous fireplace dominating one wall.

"Tempest, what a delightful surprise." Toby pushed back his chair and stood. "Do come in."

I entered the room. "Nice place you've got."

"It suits my needs." Toby looked down, and his smile faded. "I'm sorry to be the bearer of bad news, but no animals are allowed in the house. It's my allergies, you see."

I'd forgotten Toby wasn't a fan of Wiggles. I looked at him. "Are you okay to wait outside?"

"He's welcome to go in the garden, so long as he promises not to make a mess." Toby waved Wiggles back with a hand. "Feodor! We have an issue."

The huge butler appeared in the doorway.

"Take this dog outside and keep an eye on him."

"I don't need keeping an eye on," Wiggles grumbled.

"I mean, keep an eye on my plants. Some of them are valuable. I've cultivated them for years. I'd hate to see any… accidents happen."

"I don't trust the zombie butler," Wiggles muttered to me. "He might make me his next meal."

"You'll be fine. Just keep out of his reach."

Wiggles gave Toby the stink eye before turning and stomping out of the library. Feodor closed the door, leaving us alone.

"What do I owe this honor?" Toby gestured to a couch.

I perched on the edge of it. "Since things are getting serious with Aurora, it would be good to get to know each other better, just the two of us."

Toby reclined on his own couch and crossed one leg over the other. His smile looked indulgent and a little smug. "You're right to be protective of Aurora. She's a beautiful, charming woman. I know many men who are interested in her. I consider myself fortunate that she has chosen me. I adore your sister. She's delightful company, and I couldn't be happier."

"I like Aurora too. But I'm worried about how fast things are moving between you." I shifted on the couch. Despite the comfy padding, I couldn't get settled. "There's talk of you moving in together."

"There is indeed talk of such a happy event. I will welcome her into my home." Toby gestured around him. "As you see, I have plenty of space. This house has twelve bedrooms. It's too large for a single man. It's time I opened my doors to another."

"You want that other to be Aurora? You're really that serious about her?"

"I am. Your sister is flawless."

I snorted a laugh. "She's a normal person. It sounds like you've put her on a pedestal. I'd hate to see what happens if she falls."

Toby's smile faded. "I admit to a little worshipping of your sister, but that's appropriate. She has a good heart. She's generous and kind. And her beauty takes my breath away. I want to give her the best things and the best possible life."

"Her life is good as it is. She loves working at Heaven's Door, and she's got a great apartment. Plus, Aurora's surrounded by a family who loves her."

"If Aurora wishes, she can keep all of that. I will never take her from her family. And if she wants to keep her apartment, for whatever reason, she may do so."

"And her business? That's always been her focus. Aurora's not going to give that up."

Toby shrugged. "I admire ambition, but Aurora will need nothing when she's living with me. After a time, I imagine she'll find the daily grind of running a small business tedious. She'll understand that she doesn't need to do that to earn a living. I will give her everything."

"What's she going to do if she doesn't run Heaven's Door?" It sounded like Toby wanted to keep Aurora like a pet in his gilded cage.

"She'll live here. She can pursue her passions."

I narrowed my eyes. "Heaven's Door is Aurora's passion."

Toby chuckled and shook his head. "You're young and don't see the pleasures of this lifestyle. I'm sure there will be a period of adjustment as Aurora realizes all the opportunities she has. If she's insistent on keeping Heaven's Door, I'll give her the money so she can hire someone to run it. She can have that as a hobby while removing the burden."

"That's generous of you, but Aurora loves the buzz of running her store. She loves helping people. She can't do that if she pays other people to run the place."

"Does she love the stress and the early mornings? Stress does terrible things to the body. It ages a person. I don't want to see your sister fade because she's worried about anything. I can take care of it all."

This guy had Aurora's future all planned. Samantha was right. He wanted someone who'd be around to service his needs and act as his pampered housewife. That wasn't Aurora. She'd be bored out of her mind. She'd hate having no purpose other than to fluff Toby's pillows and make sure his slippers were warm.

Toby leaned forward. "My dear, have I offended you?"

"It's not me you need to worry about offending. Does Aurora know about these ambitions of yours?"

"We talk about our future a lot. She's very excited. I hope you'll be excited for us too. As my relationship with Aurora deepens, I will consider us family. I'm always generous to my family."

I wasn't buying any of this, and he couldn't bribe me into supporting this relationship. Aurora would not become Toby's house pet. She deserved better. He could charm her all he liked, but he was onto a losing game if he thought he could do the same to me.

"Would you like tea?" Toby asked.

"No, I can't stay much longer. I do have a question that's not related to Aurora. I expect you've heard about the murder at the hotel, right?"

"Yes, such a bad business. A friend of your auntie's, I believe?"

"An old friend. They used to be in the same biker gang when they were younger."

Toby pressed his lips together. "Your family is full of interesting people."

"They'll be your family too if you do commit to Aurora."

He smirked and splayed his hands. "Naturally. What do you want to ask me about this murder?"

"You know one of Auntie Queenie's other friends, Samantha Smythe-Barrow. She was also in the gang."

Toby's jaw muscles clenched, and he glanced away. "I know Samantha. We've been friends for many years. She never took the gang seriously. She used to joke about them with me."

"You're still good friends?"

"Not as close as we used to be, but we keep in touch."

"Samantha used you as her alibi for the night of Bastille's murder."

Toby nodded slowly. "Of course, she would have mentioned me. We saw each other that night but only after she insisted. Samantha and I parted a long time ago. I left her. She's a charming woman but not the right one for me."

"Because she was in a biker gang or because she liked her independence?"

Toby's nostrils flared. "A little of both. Her beauty was bewitching, and she's still an attractive older woman. But sometimes attractive features cannot overcome more fundamental character flaws. I had to let her go."

"That must have been difficult for you both."

"Samantha took it badly. I believe she still has a small crush on me." Toby rested back against his seat and flashed his brows at me.

I tried not to show how unappealing I found him. "Did you take advantage of that crush the night she came to visit?"

"The idea never crossed my mind. Samantha is a friend, but I'm not interested in her in that way."

Toby's story didn't tally with Samantha's. She'd been clear that she didn't want to be his little housewife and had left him. There'd been no talk of him ditching her, but who was telling the truth?

"What did you do when she came for her friendly visit so late at night?"

"It was late, but I'm a night owl. Samantha knows that. We had a drink, chatted about old times, and she left. Nothing happened between us. I'm with your sister now."

"Samantha said that you wanted her as a kept woman and you weren't happy when she wouldn't give up her freedom."

"Aaahhh! I see why you're so interested in my past relationship. You think I'm going to force your sister to do the same?" Toby chuckled. "Aurora's a strong-minded, smart woman. I could never convince her to do something she doesn't desire."

"So Samantha lied?"

Toby shrugged. "Memories are funny things. We change what happened in our past to fit our current beliefs. Samantha was keen on us marrying. She didn't want to work and was happy to stay at home and live a life of luxury paid for by me. She didn't make me happy, though. Samantha hides it well, but she's resentful of having missed her opportunity with me."

I barely managed to suppress a snort of laughter. Toby was grotesquely wealthy, but he was hardly a catch. He was so self-satisfied and smug that I always had the urge to slap him.

I leaned forward in my seat. "I hope your intentions toward Aurora are honorable. She's young and still has lots of living to do. I'd hate to see that stifled."

A muscle in his jaw twitched. "Your lovely sister will have all the freedom she desires. All opportunities will be available to her."

"Even if that means she won't be your stay at home housewife?"

Toby's nostrils flared again. "That's for Aurora to decide."

I sucked in a breath to continue my questioning but was hit with a wave of light-headedness. The room felt like it was spinning. I grabbed the edge of the couch, thinking I was about to topple to the floor. I squeezed my eyes shut and focused on calming my suddenly racing heart.

As I opened my eyes, a cold breeze hit me in the face. I blinked several times as I struggled to figure out where I was. The library was gone, as was Toby. I stood at the open front door of his house.

Feodor stood in front of me. "Do come again." He shut the door in my face.

I stumbled away from the door, my head pounding and my vision blurry. It felt like I'd lost time. The last clear memory I had was of grilling Toby about Aurora. Then I got dizzy and ended up outside.

Wiggles bounded around the side of the house, his front paws covered in mud. "Run! I've been spotted."

I stumbled after him, my balance still not great and my stomach churning.

"Hurry! Feodor's been chasing me for ages. I escaped when he went inside the house."

I shook my head as I staggered after Wiggles. "What did you do?"

"I dug a few holes, left a couple of presents. That will teach Toby to have allergies." Wiggles slowed as he waited for me to catch up. "You look really pale."

I looked back at the house, my vision clearing. "Something happened, but I'm not sure what. Toby gives me the creeps."

Wiggles nodded. "You'd be right to think he's creepy. And something definitely happened to you. Toby used his powers on you."

I stopped walking and stared at Wiggles. "He did what?"

"I couldn't see much because Feodor was chasing me, but I watched through the window for a minute when you were talking."

"What did you see?"

"You two having a cozy chat. It looked like it was getting tense. Suddenly, you stopped talking. You sort of froze in your seat."

I rubbed my forehead. "I don't remember that. I was grilling Toby about Aurora, and he wasn't happy about it."

"I could tell that from the sour look on his face," Wiggles said. "Anyway, Toby got up, went to his desk, came back with a pair of scissors, and cut off a piece of your hair."

I grabbed handfuls of my hair and studied it. Sure enough, there was a small amount clipped off the end. My stomach clenched, and my mouth went dry. "This is bad."

"No kidding. You need to be careful," Wiggles said. "Owning a person's hair gives them power over you. You could wind up as the next Feodor doing Toby's creepy bidding. He could turn you into his slave."

A cold shiver of worry ran down my spine. "At least this proves he's trouble. Toby used magic on me to get my hair. He's worried I'm going to turn Aurora against him." It all fell into place as my mind stopped spinning. "That's how I ended up outside the house with no knowledge of how I got there. A spell was used to compel me out."

"Then Toby's doubly creepy, especially if he can control you. Didn't Frank mind Toby messing with you?"

I checked in with Frank, but he was nowhere to be found. "I doubt he cares about Toby snipping my hair.

He probably found it funny."

"We should go back, call Toby out on his tricky behavior."

I half-turned to go back to the house. My fists clenched, but I didn't move. "He's also a liar. Toby's story doesn't tally with Samantha's. He said he dumped her and that she was free to do whatever she wanted. That's not the story Samantha gave us."

"I trust Samantha much more than Toby," Wiggles said.

I nodded. "Same here." Spending time with Toby Matlock was never on my top ten list of fun things to do, but now I had evidence to show Aurora that he couldn't be trusted. There was no way she'd stay with him after she learnt about this.

"What are you going to do about your hair? You need to get it back before Toby uses his magic on it."

"He won't do anything yet," I said. "He's got my sister in his thrall and won't want anything bad to happen to me, in case it makes her suspicious."

Wiggles cocked his head. "That could be how he's gotten Aurora so crazy about him. He's used a spell on her."

I gritted my teeth. I'd had the same concern. It was the only way this relationship made sense. "Toby would need to strengthen whatever magic he's using constantly, though. Aurora's magic eraser never leaves her throat."

"He spends a lot of time with her," Wiggles said. "That could be the reason why. If they spend too long apart, Aurora starts to see what a creepy old dude he really is."

"Let's get out of here," I said as I turned and walked away from the house. "Toby Matlock is on my hit list, but we've got another problem to focus on."

"You still need to be careful," Wiggles said. "I couldn't be certain what it was, but there are dead things buried in Toby's garden. You don't want to become the next dead thing fertilizing his roses."

A shudder ran through me. "I'll get my hair back and make sure Aurora knows not to trust him. Toby Matlock's made his first mistake and proven he's not safe to be around." I shook off the remnants of his dizzy inducing magic as we walked slowly to the hotel.

I stopped as I saw Sablo and Jophiel walk out the front door. Caprice was sandwiched between them, her head down.

"That looks like trouble," Wiggles said.

I hurried over. "What's going on?"

Caprice raised her head, tears on her cheeks. "I'm innocent."

Sablo looked at me. "We had an anonymous tip-off about Caprice."

"Tempest, they think I killed Bastille." Caprice sniffed. "I didn't do it. You know me. You tell the angels I'd never do anything to hurt Bastille."

"Are you charging her?" I asked Sablo.

"Not yet, but she's under caution, and Dazielle wants her in for questioning. The tip-off said she was about to leave Willow Tree Falls."

"I wasn't. I went to get breakfast. I took a walk to clear my head. I was still upset about last night."

"What happened last night?" Sablo asked.

I winced. "Nothing bad. Things got heated over dinner. We all want to find Bastille's killer."

"And you all thought it was me." Caprice hiccupped a sob.

"No! Not all of us." I felt guilty. Caprice's expression was one of shock and sadness. I focused on Sablo. "What evidence have you got?"

"Nothing I can discuss with you," Sablo said.

"Which means you have nothing concrete."

Sablo pursed her lips. "Which means we have a strong lead, and we're following it."

"Tempest, you have to help me." Caprice's bottom lip quivered as the angels moved her away from the hotel.

"I'll do everything I can." At that moment, I could do nothing but watch as they led Caprice toward the Angel Force headquarters.

I had my own suspicions about Caprice, but they weren't strong enough to declare her the killer. She didn't have a great alibi and had the power to kill with her fire magic, but was that enough? What was her motive?

"What do you reckon?" Wiggles asked. "Have they found Bastille's killer?"

"I'm not so sure they have," I said. "While they question Caprice, we'll keep asking questions, see if anything strange pops up. One question I'm interested in having answered is who sent in the tip-off about Caprice."

"The killer wanting to frame her?"

I nodded. "That's what we need to figure out."

Chapter 13

I walked away from the hotel with Wiggles, my mind churning over the possibility that Caprice had killed Bastille.

"We should celebrate the capture with a cake," Wiggles said.

"It's a little soon to celebrate. All we know for sure is that Caprice reacted badly when Esmeralda quizzed her about her alibi at dinner."

"And she tried to escape before the angels got her."

"Caprice must have known that fleeing would put the spotlight on her."

"She got nervous because she thought people were onto her. Caprice panicked." Wiggles nodded. "Case solved. Now, about that cake to celebrate. I'm thinking something with whipped cream."

I shook my head. "What about the anonymous tip-off? Who sent it in?"

"Someone who knew what Caprice had done."

"Someone who was in the hotel," I said, "which means someone who knew Caprice."

"You think it's someone else in the gang? One of the others saw what happened?"

I tilted my head back. "If they did, they're hiding what they know from everyone else, but why?"

"They're covering their own behind. They called in the tip-off to deflect attention and skulk away before they're caught."

"That's possible. The real killer figured out that Caprice has a lousy alibi. They stirred up enough heat, and the angels reacted and took Caprice in. When they have a prime suspect, they stop looking at anyone else."

"Which means what?" Wiggles raised a paw. "That we deserve cake?"

"No, it means we still have a killer on the loose, and the angels are wasting their time."

Wiggles lowered his paw. "It won't be the first time that's happened."

I slowed as we reached Aurora's store.

Wiggles bounded to the door. "Aurora often has treats."

I shrugged. Now was as good a time as any to speak to her about her sleazy boyfriend and make her see sense.

I pushed open the door and walked inside with Wiggles. Aurora smiled at me and gestured to the customer she served.

I wandered around, looking at the beautiful crystals and pre-made spells sitting on the shelves.

Once the store was empty, I walked to the counter. "How's business?"

"Good, as usual," Aurora said. "What brings you by?"

"Oh, you know, just seeing how my little sister's doing." I glanced at her out of the corner of my eye. "How's your love life?"

She raised her eyebrows and grinned. "Great. How's yours?"

"The same." I took a deep breath. "Have you seen Toby recently?"

"Yesterday. He came by the store. We had tea together."

"You're still into him?"

Aurora laughed as she opened a box on the counter. "Of course. He's being as lovely as ever."

"No second thoughts about being involved with a much older man?"

She tilted her head, her hair falling over her shoulder. "No. Why do you ask?"

I couldn't keep what I knew from Aurora. The more time she spent with Toby, the greater his influence would be. I needed to free her from his deceitful arms before this went too far.

"I'm not sure about him."

Aurora stopped sorting the packets of dried herbs she'd unpacked. "What makes you say that? You've only met him a couple of times, and he's been nothing but nice to you."

"I went to see him today."

"Oh! Why did you do that?"

"He's an alibi for someone in relation to Bastille's murder."

"Goodness. He never said anything about that to me. That's serious."

"Everything checked out," I said. "He's Samantha's alibi. Did you know he used to date Samantha?"

Aurora's eyebrows shot up. "I don't ask him about his past relationships. It's none of my business."

"It was serious between them."

Aurora waved a hand in the air. "Even if it was, none of that matters now. Samantha's his past, and I'm Toby's future."

"You're not at all curious what they were doing together so late that night?"

Aurora pursed her lips. "I don't know what you're insinuating."

"You think it's appropriate that Samantha was in Toby's house so late?"

"I trust Toby." Aurora shrugged. "They sound like they're old friends. I often meet with old friends and catch-up."

"After midnight, just the two of you, over a glass of wine?" I felt mean for prodding Aurora, but she needed to see Toby wasn't as honest as he made out he was.

Her face paled. "You're not going to tell me Samantha spent the night, are you?"

"No! They both said that didn't happen. They said it was just a friendly catch-up." I couldn't lie to my sister, even though it might make her doubt Toby if I did.

Aurora sighed. "There you go then. I have nothing to worry about."

"What if Toby was mean to his former girlfriends? You might like to get in touch with them and ask. It would be easy enough to talk to Samantha."

"Toby Matlock is the nicest man I know. He's well-mannered, generous, thoughtful, and sweet. If he's like that with me, he'd have been like it with his previous girlfriends. I'm just lucky no one snatched him up before I did."

"I don't know about luck," I muttered under my breath. This tactic wasn't swerving my sister from Toby. It was time to pull out the big guns. "When I was with Toby, he used his magic on me."

Aurora's eyes widened, and she dropped the packets of herbs she held. "He wouldn't do that. He has strong magic but an equally strong moral code. He never uses his ability without a person's permission."

I couldn't believe that. What was the point of being able to manipulate a person's mind if you couldn't have a little fun? I'm not talking bank robbery fun but convincing Patti to give you the biggest jam doughnut and a free treat of scones now and again, that sort of fun. Nothing that would harm another person.

"How can you be so sure?" I asked.

Aurora shook her head and scowled at me. "Did you have a late-night at Cloven Hoof? Maybe you had a few too many lemon drops. That's why you're talking such nonsense."

I choked out a laugh. "My head was clear when I spoke with Toby. We were talking about you. The next thing I know, I'm outside his house and the door gets shut in my face by his creepy butler."

"Feodor isn't creepy."

"He's seven feet tall and doesn't use words with more than two syllables. His arms are way too long for his body, and he doesn't make eye contact. He's creepy."

"He's also a big softy who adores Toby. He's been in his employment for more than a decade."

"Okay, so Feodor is a sweetie. But I'm sure Toby used his magic on me. He didn't like the fact I asked questions about your relationship."

Aurora crossed her arms over her chest. "Neither do I. Why quiz Toby about our relationship?"

"Because you're my sister, and I care about you. I'm worried you're dating someone who's not being honest. Toby's making out he's this perfect guy so he can get you under his spell."

Aurora raised a hand. "Stop right there. Toby's never used his magic on me. He never would."

I blew out a breath. "That's what I'm trying to get you to understand. You wouldn't know if he had. Toby shut me down because I was poking at something that made him uncomfortable. He's not a nice guy."

"Just because Toby doesn't ride a noisy motorbike and stroll around looking all stubbled and mysterious doesn't mean he's not a nice guy. We have different tastes, that's all."

"We're not talking about Rhett. We're talking about a guy you're threatening to spend the rest of your life with."

"Did he say that to you?" Aurora grinned at me. "Did Toby suggest he's going to ask me to marry him?"

I groaned and rubbed my forehead. "No, but that's what I'm worried about. He's got plans for you. He even suggested you give up Heaven's Door."

"Now I know you're being silly," Aurora said. "Toby likes this place. He's here most days. He knows I love the store."

"Toby's plan is to wow you with luxury and turn you into a lady of leisure." I shook my head. "You'll hate that. You'll be bored and lonely. You'll rattle around in his enormous house being watched by Feodor to make sure you behave yourself. You'll have no life of your own."

Aurora's expression hardened. "Toby's house is beautiful, and I can find plenty to occupy myself there if I do give up the store. There's the garden, the library, the pool, and plenty of rooms to choose from if I want to set up my own private spell room."

I opened my mouth to protest, but she stopped me with a shake of her head.

"No, listen to me. That's if I chose to do that, which I'm not going to do. Toby has said I don't have to work if I don't want to. I'll always choose Heaven's Door."

I snorted. "Even for a generous monthly allowance? What if Toby gives you so much money that you won't have to work?"

Aurora gestured around the store. "This isn't work. This is fun. I love helping people with their magic and giving them spells to enhance their lives. This gives me pleasure, and Toby knows that. He won't cut me off from something I love."

Toby might give Aurora his smooth talk, but I wasn't convinced. "I'm begging you not to rush into things with him. And be careful around him. His magic is really strong. He completely surprised me. It won't happen again."

"I have my magic eraser. You know I wear it all the time. Even if Toby used his magic on me, he'd constantly have to strengthen it." She rubbed the amber pendant around her neck. "I trust Toby. I'm falling in love with him."

I squeezed my eyes shut for a second. This was the worst news. I had one final card to play to convince Aurora he wasn't a good guy. "Toby did something when I was in his house."

Aurora's eyes narrowed. "What did he do?"

"Cut off a piece of my hair."

Aurora's mouth fell open. "Are you sure?"

"No, because he used magic on me. But Wiggles saw the whole thing. He was watching through the window. Toby has my hair. You don't take a lock of a person's hair for a good reason."

"You must have misunderstood." Aurora looked at Wiggles, who was flat out on his back on the rug by the store door. "What exactly did you see?"

Wiggles nodded at me as he rolled over. "What Tempest said. That old man you're dating got some scissors and took a bit of her hair. He tucked it away in his desk drawer."

"You saw that clearly?"

Wiggles scratched his belly with a back paw. "It wasn't a great view. Toby shoved me outside so I wouldn't shed fur on his shag pile carpet, and I had to keep an eye on the undead butler in case he tried to bite me, but I'm eighty percent sure that's what happened."

Aurora sighed. "You could be wrong. Maybe he was doing something else."

"Something that involved a freeze spell, scissors, and my hair?" I tapped a finger against my chin. "Maybe he's planning on buying me bows for my bonnet and wanted to make sure the colors matched my hair."

Aurora glowered at me.

"Tempest is right. You need to be wary of him," Wiggles said. "Anyone who leaves a dog in the garden rather than letting him chill on a fancy rug and eat cake has got issues to deal with."

"Toby doesn't have issues. He has allergies," Aurora said. "Wiggles, think carefully. Did you actually see him take Tempest's hair?"

My patience was wearing thin. Aurora had never doubted me like this before. "Why would I lie to you?"

"Because you don't like Toby. Because you're jealous of how happy I am with him."

"Jealous! You're dating a man old enough to be your father."

"He's refined and mature. I thought you were happy for me, but I see I was wrong."

"I'm happy for you, but I'm also worried." I reached for her hand, but she stepped away. "Think about how old Toby actually is. He dated Samantha when they were young. Samantha is in her mid-fifties. That means Toby is as well."

Aurora shook her head. "You're wrong. Toby's no older than forty."

I blinked at her rapidly. Was she kidding? She knew that couldn't be true. "Have you asked Toby his actual age?"

"I'm sure I have. He's forty."

"That's impossible. Samantha told me that Toby uses magic to look younger than his years. You're dating a really old guy."

"Tempest is right again," Wiggles said. "He's a proper old wrinkly. It's unsettling that you're into him."

"That's enough! Get out, both of you. I've had enough of being lied to." Aurora stamped to the door and opened it. "You're both nasty and spiteful. I know Toby's older than me, but I like that. He's mature, unlike the two of you."

I gaped at her. Why couldn't she see past Toby's lies? This wasn't blind love. Toby was manipulating Aurora. "I'm trying to save you from making a huge mistake."

"No, you're not. When you've gotten control of your jealous feelings, we can talk again." Aurora pointed out the door.

"You need to open your eyes. Toby is bad for you."

Aurora's cheeks colored, and her eyes sparkled with tears. "Out. Now!"

I looked at Wiggles and shrugged before we shuffled out the door, which was slammed shut behind us and the blind pulled down.

I let out a frustrated sigh. "That went well."

"Yeah, Aurora is totally going to ditch the old guy after that."

A trickle of Frank's energy curled around my spine. It seemed he was also annoyed with Toby and the influence he had over my sister.

As we walked away from Heaven's Door, Frank's energy crept further up my spine, and I felt myself grow warm. "Not now, Frank." I wasn't in the mood to deal with a jealous demon.

"I have a suggestion," he whispered. "Let me pay Toby a visit. I'll get the truth out of him. I'd enjoy pounding my fist into his face until he realizes that honesty is the best policy."

I chuckled but shook my head. "I'm tempted, but it will only make things worse between me and Aurora. If she discovers I let you loose on Toby, she might never forgive me."

"We both care about your sister in our own unique ways," Frank muttered in my head. "By getting rid of Toby, I'm showing her how much I think of her."

"We all know what you think of Aurora. Toby's being dishonest with her, but you want to choke the life out of her."

"Eventually, I will choke the life out of her. I'll enjoy holding that slender neck whilst the light fades from those pretty eyes."

I snorted. "That's never going to happen."

"It will. But before I do that, I must remove all unwelcome distractions from her life. Toby is a distraction."

"Get out of here," I growled at Frank. "If you talk about choking Aurora again, you're not getting cupcakes for a month."

He growled back twice as loud in my head before sliding down my spine.

"We need more information about Toby," I said to Wiggles.

"The angels are still investigating him. Maybe they'll share what they know."

"Not likely, but we need to check in with them and see how things are going with Caprice. While we're there, we can try getting our hands on information about what a slimeball Toby Matlock is."

"Sounds good to me. And the angels always have doughnuts in the back room."

I nodded. "And that's exactly where you need to go."

Wiggles cocked his head. "You're asking me to break into the angels' office?"

"It's important. We're saving Aurora from a terrible love match."

Wiggles snorted a cloud of sulfur. "No problem. I'll be a silent ninja hellhound, creeping into enemy territory to protect the fair maiden from the wrinkled, gnarled hands of a creepy old warlock."

"Exactly. See if you can find out what they've got on file about Toby. If Aurora isn't convinced he's bad news because of his magic tricks on me, she might be convinced when she finds out what the angels are investigating him for."

We walked the short distance from Aurora's store and into the reception area of Angel Force.

Dazielle was on the desk and nodded as I approached. "I figured you'd be by soon enough. Sablo reported that you saw Caprice's arrest at the hotel."

"I had my own suspicions about her but was surprised when you took her in. Is she talking?"

"No, but she's panicked. She'll let something slip if we keep pressing her."

"Have you got enough evidence to charge her with Bastille's murder?"

Dazielle arched an eyebrow. "Not yet, but something will turn up."

I discreetly gestured to Wiggles as I continued to talk to Dazielle.

He snuck behind the reception desk on his belly and headed toward the main office.

I had no clue how the angels filed their investigations, but if Wiggles could get a look around and see if there were files on Toby, that was a start. If

Toby was as shady as I thought he was, he'd have a whole archive dedicated to his dubious behavior.

"Are you still questioning other suspects about Bastille's murder?" I asked Dazielle. "Although Caprice was top of my list, other people could be involved."

"Caprice is our focus going forward," Dazielle said. "And I trust you won't continue to poke your nose in. I heard you've been asking questions. It's not welcome or needed."

I raised a hand. "I'm only trying to help. Bastille was a friend of the family. She was my friend."

"Which is why you shouldn't be helping." Dazielle shook her head. "I know this is tricky for you and your family. I actually expected you to be more of a problem."

"I won't be any more of a problem than I need to be, so long as you don't start pointing the finger at Auntie Queenie."

Dazielle smirked. "Queenie's got nothing to worry about."

"But her friends have?"

"They won't, so long as I get Caprice to talk. They'll be free to leave Willow Tree Falls as soon as we've charged Caprice."

"But you can't do that without enough evidence."

"Or a confession." Dazielle shrugged. "Caprice hasn't been charged with anything. She can walk out any time she likes."

"Does she know that?"

Dazielle tilted her head. "I've not expressly stated that. And if she thinks she has to be here, it gives me more time to dig."

An angel being shady with a suspect, what a shocker. I almost expected the Devil to come wandering in wearing a sparkly tutu and talking about the cold weather in Hell.

"We'll keep her for a few hours before letting her go," Dazielle continued. "Perhaps a night on her own, thinking about what she did, will make her confess."

"You don't consider Caprice a flight risk?"

"We'll keep an eye on her." Dazielle arched an eyebrow. "And, if she runs, I can always hire you to bring her back in."

"She's a witch, not a demon. I don't hunt witches." I pursed my lips. "You should keep asking around. Caprice has no real motive for wanting Bastille dead."

"How do you know that?"

I scuffed my boot on the floor. "I… well, I might have asked a few questions."

Dazielle shook her head. "Of course you did. No more. It's over. We've got the person who did this."

I couldn't let it go. I couldn't let the angels push Caprice into a confession. "Why kill Bastille at this specific reunion? Maybe that's important. What has Caprice said about this anniversary get together? It's been thirty years since the gang got together."

"Nothing. The date's not relevant."

"It could be an old grudge coming to the surface."

"No one holds a grudge for such a long time. Now that your auntie and her friends are getting on in years, I don't consider them a serious threat anymore. More a nuisance."

"They never were a threat to the village or the people living here."

"They were if you got on the wrong side of them." Dazielle tapped her finger on the desk. "I've heard stories of what they got up to."

I grinned. So had I. Auntie Queenie and her friends had been awesome in their prime and still rocked some impressive magic.

Dazielle's expression hardened. "That's not something to live up to. We have files on all of them. The Magic Council even got involved a few times to sort out their dramas."

"Okay, so they could be trouble. Getting back to Bastille's murder, it was a risk killing her at the hotel. There were other people around. She led a sheltered life and lived alone. It would have been easier to kill her in her home with no one else around."

"We're not ruling out an opportunistic killing. The women could have argued. Caprice attacked Bastille and lost control of her magic."

"What did they fight about?"

"That sounds suspiciously like a question. Something you're not supposed to be asking." Dazielle gestured to the door. "You need to leave, and I need to get back to questioning Caprice."

I glanced at the door behind Dazielle. I couldn't leave Wiggles in a building full of angels. "Any chance I can sit in on the interview?"

Dazielle snorted a laugh. "Not this time. You stick to demon hunting. I've got a new case coming your way. A real nasty piece of work. You two should get along."

Wiggles scurried out from behind the reception area and winked at me. It was time to leave.

"I look forward to it. Let me know when you hear anything useful from Caprice," I said to Dazielle.

"You're at the bottom of my list to keep informed." Dazielle lifted a sheet of paper. "Oh, my mistake. You're not even on my list."

When had Dazielle gotten so snarky? I shook my head as I left the angels to their interrogation.

I hoped they didn't stuff this up. Bastille deserved justice, and the angels had better make sure she got it.

Chapter 14

I waited until we were away from Angel Force's headquarters before speaking to Wiggles. "Did you find anything useful about Toby?"

"Nothing. These paws don't work well on filing cabinets. I had a peek on a couple of desks that were unoccupied, but they didn't have anything useful. Toby's information could be in the archive."

I pressed my lips together. I would find out about his underhanded tactics. That's all I needed, more ammunition against him to show Aurora he was wrong for her.

"Let's go to the hotel again," I said. "I want to speak to Tabitha. I didn't get a chance the other day because the angels were poking around. She might have seen something useful on the night of Bastille's murder."

Tabitha Dimples was behind the hotel reception desk when we entered. "Hi, Tempest. Any news on what the angels are doing to my guest?"

"They're keeping Caprice for questioning."

"It's a terrible business." Tabitha looked around. "Should I keep Caprice's room for her? All her things are still here. I hate to be mercenary, but I have people wanting to stay."

"How long has she paid for?"

"Another two nights."

"Keep it until then. If the angels are charging her with anything, they'll have to do it soon."

Tabitha nodded. "Do you think it was her? I'm a good judge of character and didn't get a hint of killer intent off Caprice when she checked in."

I tilted my head. "How can you tell someone's a killer?"

Tabitha took her glasses off and cleaned them. "I have a sixth sense about people. I know a good egg when I see one. I also know a rotten egg."

"What sort of egg was Caprice?"

Tabitha tutted. "An all-round good one. She's stayed here before for previous reunions and is always polite and tidy. Some guests who stay here are nothing more than pigs. The stories I could tell you about what I've found lurking under beds. Dirty pants, old socks, half-eaten sandwiches. One guest even left behind a full-sized, blow-up—"

"Were you here the night Bastille was killed?"

"Oh, yes. I don't sleep much. I have an easy chair out back, so use that to nap in. I was around on and off all night."

"Did you see anyone coming and going?"

Tabitha smiled at me. "Still doing your detective work?"

I shrugged. "I have to. You know what the angels can be like."

"A pain in the behind. They left feathers all over the carpets. It took me hours to get everything looking presentable. Did they say sorry? Of course not!"

"Have they questioned you about what you saw that night?"

"You'd think they would, but we keep missing each other. I have a business to run and can't wait around for the angels to pull their boots on and get over here." Tabitha shook her head. "Not that I want them back, messing the place up."

"I doubt they'll bother you now," I said. "They think they've got their killer."

"I suppose they know what they're doing. If you have any questions for me, ask away. I'm happy to help."

"Thanks. One of your guests, Samantha, said she left around midnight to meet somebody."

"That's right. I was in the back room and saw her leave. She returned two hours later." Tabitha arched an eyebrow. "She looked very pleased with herself. I wondered if she has a gentleman in the village and they met for a little slap and tickle. She looked disheveled when she returned if you know what I mean."

I did and wasn't happy to hear that. "Did Samantha go straight to her room after she got back from her slap and tickle?"

"She did. She couldn't see me in my easy chair. I push the recliner back so I can just see over the top of the counter when people pass. I heard her go straight up the stairs. She wears those heeled boots, so I heard them clipping on the floorboards."

"Did anything else unusual happen that night?"

"Nothing remarkable. Esmeralda called down late and asked for two mugs of cocoa. It was just after Samantha had left. I don't mind doing room service during the day, but I'd closed the kitchen, so I couldn't help Esmeralda."

"So, she didn't go to Lila's room with cocoa?"

"Oh, yes, I believe she did. I couldn't provide the drinks, but I offered her my kettle. Esmeralda was happy with that because she had her own cocoa. She came down and collected the kettle. In fact, she brought me my own mug of cocoa after making the drinks, which was sweet of her."

That was useful information. It helped to solidify Esmeralda and Lila's alibis. They were snug in Lila's room gossiping and sipping cocoa when the murder happened.

"Did anything else happen?" I asked. "The other guests said they stayed in their rooms all night."

Tabitha adjusted her glasses and tapped her fingers against her chin. "Esmeralda popped down with the kettle before she turned in, which was around two in the morning. I'd nodded off, actually, so I got a start when she appeared behind the desk. Oh, and Caprice went out."

My eyes widened. Caprice had lied to me. She'd said she'd stayed in her room all night. "What time did she go out?"

"Not long after Samantha. I wondered if they were going out somewhere together and she was running late."

"Caprice was out of her room around the time Bastille was killed?"

"Yes, but she left through the front door," Tabitha said. "That's why I didn't think anything of it."

I shook my head. "Caprice couldn't get into the garden by going out the front door and around the back?"

"Oh, no. There's not a chance of that. There's a single door to gain access into the garden, and you have to walk past reception to get to it."

"There's no side gate?"

"No. The only way Caprice could get in the garden after going out the front is to scale a fifteen-foot stone wall covered in prickly holly. I grew it up there to deter any bad sorts trying to get in."

"And if she'd done that when Caprice came back, she'd be filthy."

Tabitha nodded. "She would and most likely bloody from getting stabbed by the holly. I grow the prickles extra long."

I chewed on my bottom lip. I thought I'd found a hole in Caprice's alibi, but she couldn't have been in the garden, so why lie about going out that night?

"What about Bastille?" I asked. "When did she leave her room and go into the garden?"

Tabitha tilted her head and frowned. "That's a funny thing. I don't know. I nodded off for a while. I didn't hear the back door go, and it's a heavy wooden door, so I always hear it when it thuds shut. Bastille must have been quiet when she came down the stairs."

"What time did you fall asleep?"

"I can't say for definite. It was the early hours of the morning. I remember Samantha returning around two, so it must have been after that. I fell asleep properly after she was back and rose about six."

"And you slept in your chair all night?" I glanced over her shoulder and saw a comfortable looking pink recliner with several soft throws on it. It did look cozy.

"I always do. I like to be on hand for my guests."

So, Caprice lied about going out but couldn't have gotten into the garden. Esmeralda and Lila were in the clear because they were together the night of the murder. Samantha was having a dalliance with the sleazy Toby Matlock. That only left Auntie Queenie, and I knew she was innocent. What was I missing?

I turned away from the reception. "Thanks for the information, Tabitha."

"Is it any help?"

"It might be." I wasn't sure. Unless I could get to Caprice and find out where she'd snuck off to, I couldn't go any further with this investigation. Everyone was where they should be, and all alibis accounted for.

"Pass the information to the angels if you think it'll do them any good," she said. "I want this business sorted. That poor lady deserves justice, and I deserve not to have the angels poking around anymore and threatening my business reputation."

"We'll get to the bottom of this." I left the hotel with Wiggles, my head full of questions. I still couldn't figure out why Caprice had lied. Could she have found a way into the garden Tabitha hadn't thought of?

I checked no one was watching before sneaking around the side of the hotel.

"What are you doing?" Wiggles asked.

"Looking for a secret door." I stared at the fifteen-foot wall. There was no way I'd attempt to get over that, and Caprice had a fair few years on me.

"There's no door, but maybe a ladder would work," Wiggles said.

"It would have to be a big ladder. And Caprice would need holly resistant clothing." I eyed the sharp leaves carefully. They could do serious damage. Even if Caprice had found a way to sneak into the garden undetected, she'd have been injured.

"She could have flown."

"Caprice doesn't have that power." Not all witches were a natural on a broomstick. "I'm missing something. How did she get into the garden if she came out the front door?"

"Tabitha sounds like she sleeps on the job more than she realizes," Wiggles said. "Caprice could have snuck back in when she was snoozing. Maybe she saw Tabitha all snug in her seat and waited her out, so she couldn't see her creeping about."

"But Caprice would have needed to time it right. Otherwise, Bastille could have been waiting in the garden on her own for ages. She wouldn't have done that. If Caprice asked her to meet outside at a certain time, when she didn't show, Bastille would have gone looking for her."

Wiggles glanced at the hotel. "You don't think Tabitha's involved?"

I wrinkled my nose. "What's her motive?"

"Bastille complained about something. Tabitha's in the prime position to see everyone coming and going. She could have seen Bastille go outside and decided to get her revenge."

"It would have needed to be a serious complaint."

"Maybe Bastille saw a giant rat and threatened to call in the inspectors?" Wiggles raised his nose and sniffed. "A rat with claws and a mean expression on his face."

I shuddered. I didn't want to see any rat, big or small. "We need to focus on those who knew Bastille well. The people she trusted. The people she wouldn't think it strange to go outside with in the middle of the night. Tabitha and Bastille didn't know each other well."

"So, we're back to all of Auntie Queenie's friends," Wiggles said, "and Auntie Queenie."

I hated to do that, but there was no one else to focus on. "I need to update Auntie Queenie. She might not know that the angels have Caprice for questioning."

I turned from the hotel feeling lost. Something felt wrong about Caprice's arrest. She was an easy target because of her lousy alibi, but she'd been so stunned when the angels had taken her. It was hard to fake that.

"Time for lunch?" Wiggles said.

I nodded. "Sure, we can get lunch. Let's head to Mom's and see how everyone is." Mom would also be happy to feed us.

As soon as we arrived, Auntie Queenie bombarded me with questions before I'd even sat down. I filled her, Uncle Kenny, and Mom in on the angels' activities and wasn't surprised when Auntie Queenie didn't believe Caprice had killed Bastille.

She shook her head, her bottom lip jutting out. "I need to talk to Caprice and get to the bottom of this nonsense."

"The angels still have her. I don't know how long they'll hold her. When I spoke to Dazielle, she said they were hoping Caprice would confess because they don't have enough evidence to charge her."

"Which means she's innocent." Mom placed a fresh loaf on the table, alongside a plate of cheese and pickles, a pile of warm sausage rolls, and a mixed salad.

"The angels must let Caprice go if they don't have enough evidence," Auntie Queenie said. "Just because she was alone that night doesn't mean she's the killer. I could easily have snuck out of my bedroom once Kenny was asleep, crept to the hotel, and killed Bastille."

"Not a chance," Uncle Kenny said. "Your beautiful snoring kept me up all night."

"Oh, that was just the drink making me snore," Auntie Queenie said. "I could have done it. If the angels had a mind to, they could use that flimsy timeline to hold me, just like they're doing Caprice. They have no more evidence on her than they do me."

"Don't offer yourself as a sacrificial lamb," I said. "If you say things like that around the angels, they're dumb enough to believe you."

"There's no reason for Caprice to want Bastille dead," Auntie Queenie said.

I bit my lip. "She lied about her alibi. Caprice told me she was in her room all night, but Tabitha saw her leave after midnight."

Auntie Queenie's eyes widened and her mouth opened, but she didn't speak.

"That doesn't mean she's the killer," I continued. "There's the problem of how she got into the garden. But Caprice hid the fact she'd left the hotel. She was up to something, but I'm not certain it was murder."

Auntie Queenie sighed and pushed her plate of cheese and pickle sandwiches away.

That was a bad sign. Barely anything put Auntie Queenie off her food.

"Tempest is on the case." Mom patted Auntie Queenie's hand. "She'll figure this out."

"I'm doing my best," I said. "Until the angels find conclusive proof Caprice did this, they can't charge her. And if they do, it won't stick. Any half-decent lawyer will get her off."

"It shouldn't come to that," Auntie Queenie said. "Tempest, you have influence with the angels. They might listen to you if you plead Caprice's case. Dazielle listens to you."

"Not often," I said. "She thinks I'm interfering. I'm not able to help Caprice." But it was crucial to speak to her somehow. I had to find out why she'd lied about her alibi.

Maybe that was the missing piece of information I needed. Caprice was hiding something, and I needed to know what it was.

Chapter 15

"We've got a small party coming at nine, but other than that, it's business as usual." I stood behind the bar at Cloven Hoof, making sure everything was prepared for tonight.

Merrie Noble nodded as she walked along beside me, double checking supplies and ensuring we had enough stock. "We've got everything covered. Izzie's got the night off, so Paula and Blaze are covering. I'm here as well, so we're fine for staff."

"That's great. Have you checked the lemon drops?"

Merrie smiled. "Yes, five minutes ago, after you asked the first time."

"Sorry, of course." I was distracted by everything going on with Bastille, and my mind wasn't on the job.

Merrie's smile was sympathetic. "Are you making progress with what happened to Bastille?"

"I'm half-convinced it was Caprice but not enough to stop asking questions. Something's off about her involvement in all this."

Merrie nodded. "Don't worry about us. If there are any problems, I'll get in touch. You focus on helping Queenie and her friends."

I turned and spotted Axel Shadowsoul at the other end of the bar. He raised a glass to me as I wandered over with Merrie. "Planning to have a fun night?"

"You know me. I'm always looking for a good time." Axel was dressed all in black, which was unusual for him. His dark hair was messier than normal, and his deeply tanned skin looked less orange. In fact, he looked great.

"Make sure that good time doesn't involve any mushrooms."

He shook his head. "I learned my lesson. After I was duped by Ginger, or should I say Sandy, with that bag of mushrooms, I've gone off them. Every time I see dried mushrooms, I remember being hit with her curse."

I smiled. "That's called aversion therapy. Why didn't I think of that? All the months I spent trying to convince you to keep clean and out of trouble. All I needed to do was blast you with a couple of curses and you'd have been fixed."

Axel looked away and shrugged. "You make it sound so easy. That curse was nasty. I still wake in a cold sweat as I remember coming to underground with my mouth full of dirt and having no clue what happened."

My smile faded. Axel had been through a lot. He put on a good front of being carefree and up for a laugh, but he'd suffered when he'd been cursed by Sandy Bishop. And he was different since recovering at the hands of his demon father, Kroni. His energy had a darker vibe.

"What did your dad do to you after he took you out of Willow Tree Falls?"

"He mainly shouted at me," Axel said. "Dad told me I had terrible taste in friends. He also said I wasn't to date you. Witches and demons breeding is a bad idea."

"That's good advice," I said. "We should never breed."

Axel shrugged. "He also reminded me of my future, or my potential future, if I decide to take it on."

"He offered you a job?"

"Not yet. He doesn't think I can handle anything serious, but he has plans for me. I'm his only son."

"What about your half-sisters? They don't want in on the family business?" Axel had three half-sisters whom he rarely saw.

"Most likely. Desdemona is already involved. Foxglove and Persephone won't be far behind once they've stopped partying." He swirled his drink and downed it.

Axel had matured over the last few months. He'd only been with his dad for a couple of days while he'd recovered from the curse, but there was a more serious air about him. I couldn't decide if I liked this new version of Axel.

"Would you like another drink?" Merrie smiled at Axel.

"Always. And get one for yourself." Axel grinned at Merrie as she blushed and turned away.

I glanced from one to the other carefully. I might be wrong, but it looked like they were flirting, and Merrie was enjoying it. Merrie and Axel? I'd no idea she was interested in him.

"Am I included in that generous offer? Or are you only offering to buy Merrie a drink?" I tilted my head and grinned.

"Erm, well, no. I mean, of course, you're included." Axel scratched his chin. "I figured you'd be too busy to hang out and chat."

"Tempest's helping to solve a murder." Merrie looked at me, and her gaze shifted to the door.

"I am? I thought that was the angels' job?" My grin widened as Merrie's cheeks colored again.

"Oh, sure. I heard about the murder at the hotel." Axel nodded.

My grin faded. "I do need to get back to it. If I leave the angels to figure this out, they'll be arresting you next."

Axel's brows shot up. "I'm innocent. Whatever happened, it wasn't me."

"Sure it wasn't. Not this time. I'll leave you to it," I said to Merrie. "Be good."

Merrie turned, her gaze not meeting mine as she placed a drink in front of Axel. "I always am."

"You too, Axel. I'm watching you," I said.

He accepted the drink from Merrie. "When am I ever bad?"

I shook my head and decided not to answer that question as I left the bar with Wiggles in tow. The late shift would be about to start at Angel Force. This could be a good time to see if I could sneak in and see Caprice.

We walked through the door and over to the reception desk. Cassiel was pinning the latest Angel Force motivational posters to the walls.

I looked at the first one: *A gathering of angels can enlighten the world.*

"And leave behind a heap of feathers," I whispered to Wiggles.

Cassiel looked over at me. "Everything okay, Tempest?"

"I'm here to speak to Caprice," I said. "Has Dazielle finished with her?"

Cassiel turned. "You're too late."

My gut clenched. "Have you already charged her?"

"No, Dazielle decided we didn't have enough to charge her. She was released half an hour ago."

I let out a relieved sigh. That was a good sign. It showed the angels had been fishing for information and had nothing solid to pin on Caprice. With her free, it also meant I'd get a chance to talk to her without the angels interfering.

"Dazielle was looking for you," Cassiel said. "There's a new demon case we need your assistance with."

I turned back to the door. "She can leave the details at Cloven Hoof." The demon would have to wait. I needed to see Caprice.

I hurried to the hotel, Wiggles bounding along beside me.

Tabitha walked in from the garden as we arrived, carrying a bucket and sponge. "Tempest, back so soon. I'll have to get you your own room."

"I heard Caprice has been released. I hoped I'd find her here," I said.

"Oh, of course. Yes, she came back not long ago. The poor thing looked tired. She said she was going to lie down and then head out to get some dinner. I asked if she needed anything, but she said she was fine. It looks like she's innocent though since the angels let her go."

"Quite possibly," I said.

Tabitha's expression grew cautious. "She is innocent, isn't she? I'm not having a killer in my hotel. I've just been scrubbing the burn marks off the paving slabs out back."

"I'm sure she's safe. I've known Caprice for years. And the angels have let her go, so they can't be too concerned. Is it okay if I go up?"

"Yes. She'll appreciate a friendly face." Tabitha peered into her bucket. "I need to find something stronger to get rid of the burn marks. Or I could move a pot plant over the place, hide any signs of, well, you know, what happened."

I nodded as I headed to Caprice's room and knocked on the door. There was no reply. I knocked several more times.

"Maybe she's asleep," Wiggles said, "or in the shower washing off the angel stink."

I tried the handle of the door, and it opened. I glanced down at Wiggles. "What do you think? If she's asleep, we can sneak out and come back later."

"Fine by me. I can be stealthy when I'm searching for panties to chew on."

I glared at him.

"Fine, no panties."

I eased open the door, crept inside, and pushed it shut behind me. There was a small private bathroom to the left and, in front of me, a short corridor with a fitted wardrobe. The bedroom was in the main room.

I tiptoed toward the bed. It was empty. There was no sign of Caprice.

The room was also a mess. A chair had been knocked over and the bedding tossed around.

"Where's she hiding?" Wiggles trotted to the bed and peered underneath. "She's not under there."

A quick check of the bathroom showed it was just as empty.

I opened the closet. "Her case has gone."

"Caprice is making a run for it," Wiggles said. "She's guilty and sees this as her only chance to escape."

I looked around the room, disappointment flickering through me. I didn't want to believe she was the killer. "She's left a lot of things behind." There was a makeup bag in the bathroom, a pair of what looked like designer boots by the door, and several cosmetic items dotted around.

"She had little time," Wiggles said. "Caprice grabbed what she could and made a run for it."

"We should let the angels know. If she's escaping, she won't have gotten far." I hurried back to the reception and told Tabitha what I'd discovered.

Her eyes were wide as she scratched her head. "How strange. I didn't see her leave."

"You were in the garden when we arrived. She must have left then."

"Caprice must have been waiting for me to turn my back so she could escape. I'm glad I did. If she's desperate for a way out, she could be dangerous. She could have hurt me."

"You need to send a message on the snow globe and let the angels know what's going on."

"Of course. I'll do it right away." Tabitha bustled away and returned a moment later. "They're on their way. They said for you to wait here."

It only took five minutes before Dazielle arrived. She fluttered her wings into place as she strode through the door. "Tempest, what a surprise. You're snooping."

"There's no time to nag me. Something's going on with Caprice. Things are missing, and her room's a mess."

"Let's take a look before you go leaping to conclusions." Dazielle led the way back up the stairs and into Caprice's room. She stood for a moment looking around. "My team is on the lookout for

Caprice. We'll search the village and spread out wider if there's no sign of her. I didn't think she'd flee. She seemed reasonable and promised she was staying put."

Worry churned in my gut. There was something about the mess in the room, and the way things had been thrown about that unsettled me. "Caprice is always immaculate."

"Tempest, she's a fugitive. When you're under stress, you act out of character. Did you expect her to make the bed and fold the towels before going on the run?"

"No, but look at the bedding. It's shoved on the floor. The bed would have been made since this morning." I looked around some more. "And Caprice left behind designer boots that cost a lot of money."

Dazielle stared at the boots and shrugged. "She can do without her designer clothes. They'll be no use to her when she's behind bars for murder."

I walked around the other side of the bed. On the floor was a broken lamp. This room wasn't the scene of someone fleeing in a hurry. This was the scene of someone who'd been fighting.

Tabitha knocked on the door and opened it. "I don't like to disturb you, but there's a message for Tempest from Suki."

I walked to the door. "Did she say what's wrong? Is it a problem at Cloven Hoof?"

"No, but she sounded upset. She said something's been found in the forest."

"Did she say what it was?"

"She's coming here to tell you herself." Tabitha glanced at Dazielle. "It sounded important."

"You go," Dazielle said. "I can handle things here."

I looked at the mess in the room. "Caprice was taken. She's not running. I think she's in trouble."

Dazielle pursed her lips. "And you know that how?"

"This is the scene of a fight. Messy bedding, a broken lamp, things missed when hurriedly packing a case to make it look like Caprice is on the run."

Dazielle studied the room again. "I'll get my team to do a sweep and see if they find anything unusual."

There was nothing more I could do to convince Dazielle there was something odd going on. I hurried down the stairs and out the front door of the hotel with Wiggles.

Suki was racing toward me from the direction of Cloven Hoof, waving her hand as she spotted me.

She stopped as she reached me and gasped in air. "I have terrible news."

"What's wrong?" I'd never seen Suki look so pale. "Is there a problem with magic in the forest?"

"Fallon found something," she gasped.

"What did she find?"

"A body," Suki said. "She found a body hanging from a tree."

I took a step back, my heart racing. "Does she know who it is?"

"No, she didn't recognize them. She said it's an older woman, well put together. Fancy clothes."

My heart skipped a beat. That sounded like Caprice. "Wait right here." A raced back into the hotel and up the stairs. "Dazielle! I think Caprice is in the forest."

She appeared from out of the bedroom. "Let's get after her."

"Wait!" I grabbed her arm as she hurried past me. "There's a problem. She might be dead."

Dazielle blinked rapidly. "Dead? Are you sure?"

"No! Come with me." I led her outside to speak to Suki.

Suki confirmed what Fallon had found and where the body was, her worried gaze returning to me as she spoke with Dazielle.

Dazielle let out a sigh. "Very well. Let's go take a look." She took flight and headed toward the forest.

I raced after her with Suki and Wiggles. My stomach was churning with worry and my nerves jangling. Would Caprice do something as drastic as this? She would if she was guilty and it had gotten too much for her to bear.

We hadn't gone far before Fallon popped out from behind a tree, her dark eyes bright with excitement. "Greetings, forest visitors."

"Fallon, where is she?" I asked.

"Right this way." Fallon gestured us to follow her along a narrow path.

We rounded a tree, and I gasped. It was Caprice. And she was very dead.

Dazielle alighted on the ground and came to stand next to us. She stared up at Caprice before shaking her head. "Suicide."

It looked like it. "She must have been guilt-ridden over what she did to Bastille."

"Has anyone checked for a pulse?" Dazielle asked.

"I have." Fallon pushed past me. "Forest Guardian at your service. I shimmied up the tree and checked. She's gone, but she's not been here long. She's still warm."

I looked away and swallowed. I didn't like encountering dead bodies, especially not ones swinging from a tree, and especially not when they were people I knew and cared about.

"She must have been desperate to do this," Suki said quietly. "She must have felt she had nowhere else to turn. I'm so sorry, Tempest." She placed a large hand on my arm.

I blinked away tears. "Thanks."

"I'll bring in reinforcements," Dazielle said. "We'll get Caprice down."

It only took a few minutes before two more angels descended from the sky. They got to work and carefully removed the rope from around the tree branch and placed Caprice on the ground.

As much as I didn't want to, I inched over to take a look.

"She must have broken her neck when she jumped off the branch," Dazielle said. "It would have been quick. It doesn't look like she suffered."

I leaned closer, focusing on the rope around Caprice's neck. "Does rope make burn marks like that?"

"Stay out of the way, Tempest," Dazielle said sharply. "I appreciate the information about Caprice's location, but there's nothing you can do."

"But look at her throat," I said, my pulse hammering, making my head hurt. "Under the red marks, it looks like her skin's been burned."

Dazielle's head jerked back before she drew closer. "It's hard to tell. Maybe it's bad friction burns from the rope."

I didn't believe that. The marks were subtle, but they were there. "Wiggles, get over here."

Wiggles bounded over. "What do you need?"

"You saw Bastille's neck. Do the marks on Caprice look similar?"

"Your hellhound isn't an expert in identifying the cause of death," Dazielle said.

"But he saw both bodies." I nodded at Wiggles. "What do you think?"

He sniffed the body. "It's the same smell. Chargrilled chicken. Caprice was burned before she died."

I nodded. "Someone choked her with flaming hands and hid the evidence by staging her death as a suicide."

"Caprice was murdered too?" Suki clutched my shoulder.

"Yes. Whoever did it must have hoped the rope marks would conceal the real cause of her death."

"There's a vague possibility that happened." Dazielle stared at the body for several seconds. "We'll get her back and do a more thorough investigation, without your input."

"This wasn't suicide," I said. "Caprice was murdered."

Chapter 16

I'd spent the last few hours in a daze. I'd gone through the motions of eating dinner and staring blankly at paperwork in the back office of Cloven Hoof, but I was in shock. Caprice was dead. She'd not committed suicide. Someone had wanted her out of the way.

After Dazielle and her team had poked around for a while, even they agreed her death was suspicious.

I was certain that Bastille and Caprice had been killed by the same person. That person had tried to frame Caprice for Bastille's murder and make it look like she'd ended her life because she was so torn up about murdering her friend.

I shoved the paperwork to one side and rested my head in my hands.

Wiggles' head appeared on my knee. "How's it going?"

I stroked his ears. "Not great. Who's doing this?"

He nuzzled my hand with his muzzle. "A mean person whom we're going to catch. I'm going to bite them so hard when we do. I love these witches. No one gets to bump them off."

"Me too. We have to figure this out." The problem was, I had no idea where to look next.

"I need some air." I left the office, and after a quick check-in with the bar staff, I headed out of Cloven Hoof. I couldn't process everything I'd witnessed, so maybe a change of scene would help.

It had gone eleven at night, but there was no way I could think about settling down for the night.

I wandered the streets with Wiggles by my side, not going in any particular direction. There had to be something bigger behind this, something I'd missed. The only connection between Caprice and Bastille was their old biker gang affiliation. Was that it? Was that why they'd been killed? Someone had an old grudge that they'd finally decided to act on?

I stopped when I saw a warm, welcoming amber light on in Tilly's restaurant. She was closing Bite Me for the night, and the place was empty.

I walked over and knocked gently on the glass door. A moment later, Tilly appeared, still in her apron. She waved at me and hurried to open the door.

"Hey! I meant to catch up with you. I heard about what's going on with Queenie's friends. How horrible." She ushered me inside and locked the door behind me and Wiggles.

"Have you heard the latest?" I asked.

"All I know is that Bastille was killed at the hotel, and the angels have Caprice in for questioning." She rested her hands on her hips. "What have I missed?"

I slumped into a seat and dropped my head into my hands. "There's more. None of it good."

"Hold those thoughts." Tilly patted my shoulder. "This needs pie and strong coffee."

"For me too," Wiggles said. "Although I'll take a bowl of milk with my pie."

Tilly narrowed her eyes. "You shouldn't even be here, but I sense this is a crisis situation. You can stay, so long as you behave yourself."

Wiggles raised a paw and cocked his head. "I'll be a good boy."

"Thanks, Tilly, you're a lifesaver," I said.

Tilly returned a moment later with a tray. There were three pieces of pumpkin pie with ice cream, a bowl of milk, and a pot of coffee with a plunger. She placed a plate down for Wiggles before setting the rest out for us. She poured the coffee and settled in her seat.

I took a few sips of coffee. "Caprice didn't kill Bastille. I'm certain of it."

"What makes you say that?" Tilly cut a piece of her pie, swirled it in some melting ice cream, and took a bite.

"We found Caprice in the forest this evening, hanging from a tree."

Tilly choked on her pie as she dropped her spoon. "Suicide?"

"It looked like it at first, but whoever put her there did a lousy job of covering their tracks. She was killed the same way as Bastille. The hanging was a cover. I'm no forensic expert, but I only needed to look for a minute before I spotted something was wrong with how Caprice died."

"I'm so sorry to hear that. Who did this?" Tilly sipped her coffee.

"I can't figure it out." I shook my head. "But I don't believe Caprice killed Bastille. What concerns me is that someone could be picking off Auntie Queenie's old biker gang one at a time, but I don't know why."

Tilly's brow furrowed. "Tempest, this is worrying. Does Queenie know?"

"I can't face telling her, not yet. I'm still in shock, but it won't be long before word spreads, so I'll have to see her soon and break the news. I'll do it first thing in the morning."

Tilly's mouth twisted to the side. "Could Queenie be at risk?"

I jerked back in my seat. "The killer wouldn't dare try anything with Auntie Queenie."

"I'm sure you're right. She's one tough cookie. If anyone did try anything, they'd be sorry."

"She's safe for now. Uncle Kenny and Mom are with her in the house." Even so, with this concern added to my list, I had to decide on my next move and fast. No one went after a member of my family and got away with it.

I cut a piece of my pie and ate it. This was just what I needed, a friend, great food, and strong coffee to help get my thoughts in order.

"There is one thing playing on my mind. Caprice lied about her alibi. She said she was in her room the night of Bastille's murder."

Tilly jabbed her spoon at me. "I can tell you straight up that's wrong. I was clearing up late that night. I'd had a private party in for a fiftieth birthday celebration. They were late leaving, which I didn't mind, they spent a lot of money on after-dinner drinks. I was clearing the last table when I saw somebody walk past. It was Caprice."

I sat up straight. "Was she alone?"

"She was. I almost went out after her because I thought she looked in pain. She was clutching her stomach. At first, I thought it must be cramps but then remembered Caprice is a bit old for cramps."

"Caprice didn't mention feeling unwell when we had the party in the forest. Maybe it was something she ate."

"Whatever it was, perhaps she thought fresh air would make her feel better. Caprice could have forgotten she went for a walk that night, what with the shock of Bastille's murder."

"Or she was worried she'd be taken in for questioning. Caprice went out alone and had no alibi. It looks suspicious. Now, I can't get any answers from Caprice about what she was doing that night."

"If it wasn't Caprice, who do you think killed Bastille?"

"Everyone has an alibi. We'll have to start over and figure out where people were when Caprice died. I must speak to Auntie Queenie as well. Maybe she'll remember an old enemy who's out for revenge. Someone we've overlooked."

"But why now?" Tilly asked. "Why has this mysterious enemy resurfaced after such a long time?"

"If there even is one." I raised my hands, feeling exasperated. I felt like I was clutching at straws, and those straws kept slipping through my fingers.

Tilly smiled. "More pie?"

"Not for me," I said.

"Yes, please," Wiggles said.

"One piece is enough for a little guy like you." Tilly scooped up the empty plates and sat them on the counter.

"I need my strength to help fight crime," Wiggles said, his hopeful gaze on the empty plates.

"You've got plenty of reserves." Tilly poked his belly. "You live off that for a while."

I fiddled with my mug of coffee. "There's also another mystery I need your help with. It's not related to these murders."

Tilly turned from the counter. "What's that?"

"Toby Matlock, what do you know about him and Samantha? I've learned they used to date. I think they might still have some sort of relationship."

"Samantha and Toby!" Tilly returned to her seat, a mischievous look on her face. "I thought Toby liked his women much younger these days."

I narrowed my eyes. "What do you know about Toby's dating situation?" I didn't know how widely Aurora had shared her secret relationship and wasn't going to reveal anything.

Tilly smiled. "I don't want to get anybody in trouble, but I've seen Toby with a younger woman. She's very pretty and extremely sweet. We both know her."

I tilted my head. "Is she a local business owner whom I'm related to?"

"You do know about Toby and Aurora!" Tilly smacked the back of my hand. "I've been desperate to say something but didn't know how hush hush their relationship is."

"It's very hush hush," I said. "No one else in the family knows. How did you find out?"

"They were very discreet when I saw them together. If I didn't know your sister so well, I'd think she was just being friendly to Toby, but it was the way he touched her arm and gazed at her. I knew then something was going on between them. They're really in a relationship?"

"They are." I pressed a finger to my lips. "Don't say anything to anybody else."

"But that guy's ancient. He's old enough to be my father."

"The age thing isn't even the biggest issue. There's something off about Toby." I recounted my recent meeting with him and what he did to me.

Tilly was horrified. "You're right to be concerned if he's misusing his power. Toby will be in big trouble if he gets found out, even more so if you think he's seeing Samantha behind your sister's back."

"I don't know that for definite, but their stories are different. I'm concerned something happened between them that night. If that's the case, then Toby's cheating on Aurora. Aurora should know, but I don't think she'll listen to me."

"And, not forgetting, Toby used powerful magic on you without your consent," Tilly said. "Aurora isn't worried about that?"

"She's too love-struck to be worried. She can't see a flaw in Toby. Aurora also thinks he's much younger than he is." I swirled the last of my coffee around. "What if he's using magic on Aurora to make her think he's this amazing guy? He could be influencing her mind so she becomes besotted with him."

"When I saw them together, Aurora seemed genuinely interested. She was laughing and smiling. I've never seen her so happy with a guy. I'll admit it's weird and a bit gross to be going out with someone that old, but opposites attract. Your sister is lovely, and Toby is a rich, older guy who can show her the world if that's what she wants."

"I'm not buying it. He's a creep, and I won't be happy until he's far away from Aurora."

"Be careful, Tempest," Tilly said. "If your sister is as crazy about him as she sounds, you risk driving her away if you say anything against Toby. You know what it's like when you're in love. It doesn't matter what anybody says, you only see the good things. So, tread carefully."

"I've already put my foot in it," I said. "I do owe Aurora an apology. But Toby's still not having her."

Tilly tilted her head from side to side. "Have you thought about setting Frank on him?"

I laughed. "For once, you and Frank are in agreement. He suggested that himself. He thought it would be fun to pay Toby a visit and pound the truth out of him."

"It's not a terrible idea," Tilly said. "Although, just some scaring rather than any physical violence. I'm not a fan of Toby Matlock, and his ability gives me the shivers. If he's manipulating your sister, it has to be stopped."

I leaned back in my seat as I finished my coffee.

It felt like there were too many puzzles and problems to solve, and I had no way to sort any of them.

Chapter 17

I was up uncharacteristically early the next day.

I left Wiggles sleeping on my bed and headed to Angel Force. I waited a few moments in the reception until Dazielle came through.

"Any news on Caprice?" I asked.

"Nothing good," Dazielle said. "Your suspicions were right. Once we'd examined the body, there were clear burn marks. They were more discreet than the ones we found on Bastille."

"Because the real killer tried to make Caprice's murder look like a suicide. Whoever it is used Caprice as a fall girl."

"That's what we're thinking," Dazielle said. "The killer must have waited for Caprice to be released after we questioned her. They pounced as soon as she got back to the hotel."

"Have you checked with Tabitha? Did she see anyone lurking around or watching the hotel?"

"She didn't see anything odd," Dazielle said. "But it wouldn't have been hard for someone to sneak in and attack Caprice."

"But not so easy to take her to the forest. They'd have had to carry her body."

"Unless they forced her using magic," Dazielle said.

"Caprice was an elemental witch. It would have taken a powerful magic user to bring her down without a struggle."

"There were signs of a fight in her room."

"Yes, that I spotted. Before you did."

Dazielle arched an eyebrow. "Congratulations. We also found Caprice's suitcase in the forest. It was hidden under a bush."

"The killer took some of her things to make it look like she was leaving but then changed their mind?"

"Or they wanted to complicate matters. If Fallon hadn't found Caprice in the woods, we'd have been searching elsewhere."

I nodded. "Giving the actual killer time to escape."

"That could be true."

"I don't think Caprice was killed in her room. We'd have detected the smell of burning. I reckon the killer knocked her out, which explains the struggle in the room, cloaked them both, and took Caprice into the forest to kill her, where there'd be no interruptions."

"That's possible," Dazielle said.

"But they didn't do a great job," I said.

"Agreed, it was an amateur job. Possibly an opportunistic killing. We're going to speak to everyone again to see what they know." Dazielle tilted her head. "And, as a courtesy, I'll let you know we will be talking to Queenie. She has an alibi for the first murder, but we need to know where she was when Caprice was killed."

I gritted my teeth and nodded. "I won't stand in your way. Somebody saw something. There are other guests in the hotel, and they could have seen someone go to Caprice's room."

Dazielle shuffled the papers on the reception desk. "You're being surprisingly cooperative."

"So are you. You could have told me nothing about Caprice."

Dazielle raised a hand as if to pat my arm but then scratched her wing instead. "I understand this is difficult for you. People you know and care about are dying."

"And you don't think I'm doing the killing?"

Her eyes narrowed. "Don't push your luck. My sympathy has an expiry date."

I shrugged. I did appreciate her letting me know what the angels were doing. "You're not forbidding me from seeing Auntie Queenie?"

"No. I would ask that you don't discuss our investigations, but I'll be wasting my breath. Just be discreet. We're still looking for a killer."

"Will do." I nodded goodbye and headed to Mom's house. I needed to get to Auntie Queenie before the angels did and let her know what happened to Caprice. As usual, the front door was open.

I slowed as I walked into the hallway. There were hushed voices coming from the kitchen. I recognized Auntie Queenie, and I was pretty sure the other person was Lila.

"We can't mention this to anybody just yet," Auntie Queenie said.

"I think we should. This could be the reason we're being targeted." Lila's tone was tense. "I've been feeling terrible recently, and nothing is helping."

"You're not as bad as Bastille was. She got the brunt of that foul magic."

I inched closer to the kitchen door. What were they talking about?

"I wasn't far away from her," Lila said. "It took me several months before I could even get back on my feet."

"I've got something to fix you up if you're not feeling so good," Auntie Queenie said.

I didn't know Lila was also sick. It seemed like every member of the gang had some kind of ailment.

"We should share this information with the angels," Lila said. "If we give them this book, they might help."

"Help how? They can't undo the magic, and we can't go accusing anyone on the Magic Council of coming after us."

My eyebrows shot up. The Magic Council was after Auntie Queenie and her friends? What for?

"I'm worried," Lila said. "This feels serious. Whoever is doing this means business. What if they don't stop until they've wiped us all out?"

"It won't come to that. Let's get some fresh herbs from the garden for your tonic," Auntie Queenie said. "Until we know more, we can't do anything. If we tell the angels our concerns, they'll flap around and have no idea what to do. It'll only make it worse. We don't need them to know about our pasts. They might lock us up if they do."

Their pasts? What had they done that was so bad the angels would put them behind bars?

I waited until I heard them leave the kitchen through the back door and hurried into the room. Sitting on the table was a small black book. I flipped it open. There were dates and details of different magical items, their side-effects, and a power listed against each one. The pages were old, and several were stained. I had no idea what I was looking at.

Whatever it was, it sounded like it had gotten Auntie Queenie and her former biker babes into trouble with the Magic Council.

The Magic Council generally kept to themselves. They ran the administrative side of magic. They issued laws regarding magic use, monitored infringements, and used their significant influence to curb dangerous magic and ensure the checks and balances were in place so nobody became too powerful.

I turned the page of the book and trailed my finger down it. This had all kinds of magic listed but not the names of the item or spell. All of it sounded powerful and a little warped. There were initials next to an item that could turn you mad, another set of initials listing a power that forced a person to speak the truth, and something that compelled a person to do anything you commanded them.

This could just be a record of all the magic the gang had access to over the years, but it sounded like something else was going on. Something that involved deadly spells and curses.

I continued to read. From the details in the book, it looked as if this magic was tested to see how effective it was and what harm it did. The side-effects were listed, and there was a color next to each spell. A red, amber, or green dot.

"What does this mean?" I muttered to myself as I sifted through the pages, looking for an explanation of the code.

"The code means safe, be careful, and destroy at once." Auntie Queenie stood in the door leading out to the garden. Lila was next to her.

I shut the book swiftly. I'd been so engrossed I hadn't heard them come back. "What's this about?"

Auntie Queenie rubbed her forehead as she placed the herbs she'd collected onto the table. "Here's a tricky thing. What can we tell you?" She glanced at Lila.

Lila pressed her lips together and nodded. "Tempest is involved. She might be able to help."

"Help with what?"

"Sit down both of you. I'll make this tonic," Auntie Queenie said.

Lila sank gratefully into a seat. She looked pale, and there was a gray tinge to her skin. It could be because of the shock of recent events, but I had a feeling it was more than that.

"If you're here to tell us about Caprice, we already know." Auntie Queenie swiftly chopped the herbs and placed them in a pestle before grinding them.

Lila shook her head. "Terrible news."

"Oh! Yes, I was coming to tell you that." In my surprise at finding this mysterious book, I'd forgotten my purpose for visiting. "How did you find out?"

"I was in the bakery late yesterday. Patti saw the angels fly to the forest. The rumor mill got going before the day was out." Auntie Queenie paused to dab her eyes. "We still can't believe it. Another sister has fallen."

Guilt filtered through me. It was a lousy way to find out. "Sorry, I should have told you as soon as I knew."

Auntie Queenie patted my hand as she sniffed back tears. "I understand. You're figuring this out. You've got a lot going on. What do the angels think happened?"

"It wasn't a suicide. It's the same person who killed Bastille. I'm almost certain."

Lila's hands fluttered to her chest. "I knew it. They're after us."

I waited a minute for either of them to elaborate on what that meant, but neither spoke. "Auntie, what's going on? Who's after you, and what does it have to do with this book?"

"The book is a record." Auntie Queenie tipped the herbs into a mug, poured hot water over them, sprinkled in some magic powder, and handed the mug to Lila. "Drink that and you'll get color back in those cheeks."

Lila nodded and took a sip. "Thanks, it's just what I need."

Auntie Queenie finally sat at the table and clasped her hands together. "You know I was part of the Dead Tree Witch gang."

"Of course, you all were."

"I've always talked about the gang as if it was a bit of fun. A chance for me to hang out with my friends, ride around on fancy bikes, and enjoy ourselves." She glanced at Lila. "It was a bit more than that. When you get such powerful magic users together, you can do impressive things."

I nodded. Everyone knew that a coven of witches could share power and strengthen a spell when they worked together. "What sort of things did you do?"

"It was nothing bad," Lila said quietly. "But our combined ability came to the attention of the Magic Council. They called upon our services."

I looked at the book. "They gave you these magic items and spells to test?"

"Exactly," Auntie Queenie said. "Here's the tricky bit. We were sworn to secrecy by the Magic Council. We can't talk about what we did."

"You can tell me anything," I said. "I won't say a word."

"You misunderstand. We literally cannot talk about it. If I try to discuss the magic in that book with anyone outside of the group, I won't be able to. My voice vanishes."

I blinked at her rapidly. "The Magic Council put a spell on all of you?"

"That's right," Lila said. "We were handling dark magic. They decided it was too much of a risk if we could talk freely. We can talk to each other about it, but that's it. If anyone else is in the room, we go mute."

"However, the Magic Council aren't as smart as they think," Auntie Queenie said. "They didn't say we were forbidden from writing our results down. I kept a record. It was partly so it was easier to report back to the Council and tell them what we'd discovered, but I was also curious. We tested so much magic over the years that I couldn't remember it all."

"So, what's the problem? Is the Magic Council not happy that you have this book?"

"We worked with them for almost a decade," Auntie Queenie said. "There was no problem until their requests changed and we became uneasy with their demands."

Lila ducked her head. "They asked us to use the magic on specific people."

I jerked back in my seat. "They wanted you to be magic using assassins?"

"Nothing that sophisticated," Auntie Queenie said. "We were happy to test the magic and use it within a protective circle when together, but we never used it on our own. There's power within those pages. For a single witch to use such power, it would kill her."

"We didn't turn the Council down to begin with," Lila said. "We targeted the magic on a few people, as they requested."

"At first, it wasn't an issue." Auntie Queenie lowered her head. "It wasn't until someone died from the magic we used that we stopped helping the Magic Council."

"They got you to kill someone?"

"They claimed it was an accident. The magic should never have killed the target." Lila frowned. "The individual had been weakened by other magic they were unaware of."

"After that, we said no more to using magic on others," Auntie Queenie said. "We were prepared to continue testing magic, and the Council agreed we could do that. Everything was fine for a few months. We still got magic sent our way and reported our findings."

"Until an item backfired," Lila said. "We were sent a corrupted potion. When we activated it, it attacked us."

My eyes widened. "How did it affect you?"

"It made everyone sick, some more than others," Lila said.

"I've always suspected the Magic Council used that potion to try to get rid of us," Auntie Queenie said. "We knew too much and had stopped following their orders. And we'd used magic under their instruction against others. If we decided to reveal what we'd done, the Magic Council would have been in trouble."

Lila tilted her head. "We have no proof. The potion could have gone wrong. Magic distorts over time or when it's not handled correctly."

"We know how to handle magic," Auntie Queenie said. "This wasn't a problem of our making. Everyone who was there when that potion activated got sick. Basically, the whole of the Dead Tree Witch gang."

"Did this potion make Bastille sick?" I asked.

"Yes, she was closest to the potion when it activated," Auntie Queenie said.

"And I heard from Tilly that Caprice didn't seem well on the night of Bastille's murder." I glanced at Lila. "You also don't look too good."

Lila sighed. "I've felt better."

I grabbed Auntie Queenie's hand. "What about you? Did this potion get on you?"

She patted my hand. "I was the lucky one. I wasn't there when the gang used the potion. I returned to find them weak and sick. It took them months to recover. By then, the gang was on its knees. That's when we were driven out of Willow Tree Falls by a rival gang. We disbanded not long after."

I let out a sigh of relief. Auntie Queenie was safe from whatever this potion was doing to the others. "Did the witches you commemorated at the dinner also get affected by the potion?"

"They were there." Auntie Queenie's eyes widened. Her worried gaze went to Lila. "You don't think…"

"They died because that potion weakened them?" Lila's eyes filled with tears. "That can't be true."

"When you told me about their deaths, I thought it was odd," I said. "Four healthy witches dying within two years of each other."

"When they returned from their travels, they were sick, so we assumed it had to be related to something they came into contact with when they were away, not the potion," Lila said.

Auntie Queenie dabbed at her eyes with a tissue. "They thought their trip would help them recover. They wanted to have some fun and forget about their worries."

"Maybe the Magic Council found a way to kill them without making it look like murder," I said.

"As they tried to do with Caprice." Auntie Queenie's chin lifted a slight wobble in her jaw. "I've never thought about it until now. What if that potion weakened them over time? Then they activated something dark when they were on their travels. The Magic Council realized they were vulnerable, so they took the opportunity to take them out."

"It can't be the Magic Council doing this," Lila said. "They're not perfect, but they aren't assassins."

I sat back in my seat. "If this is the reason behind the murders, it means nobody in your group is the killer. Someone else is after you because of what you know or what you did to them."

"We're being picked off one by one by someone who knows what we did for the Magic Council," Lila whispered.

"Or by the Magic Council themselves. They've realized we know too much," Auntie Queenie said. "They consider us a liability. Our relationship with the Magic Council isn't great."

"I still can't believe it's the Magic Council coming after us," Lila said. "They're a bunch of officials sitting in their fancy offices, and we can't talk about any of the magic we tested. We're no threat."

I nodded. It also seemed unlikely to me that the Magic Council would take out Auntie Queenie and her friends. "Could it be somebody you used the magic on?"

"It's most likely somebody who's magic was taken for us to experiment with," Lila said. "Those powerful spells and magic-filled items came from other magic using creatures."

Auntie Queenie nodded. "The Magic Council had a push two decades ago and cracked down on lethal spells, forcibly removing them from magic users."

"And one of those magic users now wants revenge against you." This was the worst possible news. Somebody was targeting every member of the Dead Tree Witch gang, including Auntie Queenie.

She took hold of my hand and squeezed it. "This killer isn't messing around. Don't put yourself at risk to help a bunch of middle-aged women who played with fire when they were younger. We can sort this ourselves."

There was no way I'd leave them to figure this out on their own. "I'm going nowhere."

"What are we going to do?" Lila looked at me as she spoke.

I reached for her hand and linked us together. "Find out who it is before they strike again and stop them."

215

Chapter 18

After learning about Auntie Queenie's association with the Magic Council, I decided to assemble the remaining gang members at Mom's house. Together, they should be able to figure out who most wanted them dead.

We'd arranged for Esmeralda and Samantha to come by at lunchtime, but every other member of the family had been excluded. The fewer people who knew what was going on, the better. I didn't want anyone else added to this killer's hit list.

Aurora was working at the store, so she wouldn't be a problem. Granny Dottie and Mom were taking a shift at the cemetery, so they couldn't be involved.

I gently shooed Uncle Kenny and Grandpa Lucius out the front door just before noon. "We're having a girls' afternoon. No men allowed."

Grandpa Lucius looked at me with suspicion in his eyes. "Since when do you organize girls' afternoons?"

"Starting today," I said.

"What about your sister? She's a girl, and I don't see her here."

"She's busy." I smiled at him. "Don't come back for several hours, unless you want your nails painted and a clay mask applied."

Uncle Kenny chuckled as he backed away. "Don't worry. We've got a couple of seats waiting in the Ancient Imp."

Grandpa Lucius kissed my cheek, his narrowed gaze suggesting he didn't entirely believe me. "Have fun."

They strolled out of the gate and along the lane. I didn't like keeping secrets, but it was better for them if they didn't know what we were involved in. Safer for them.

I raised a hand as I saw Samantha hurrying toward me. She looked flustered, and her cheeks were flushed. I briefly wondered if she'd made a detour to see Toby, but I couldn't worry about her tangled love life now. We had a killer to find.

"The message from Queenie was most mysterious." Samantha stopped beside me. "What's going on?"

"We've got an idea about who killed Bastille and Caprice," I said. "We have to be discreet. The fewer people who know, the better."

"Oh, goodness." Samantha took a step back. "Fair enough. I've just finished talking to the angels again. They're grilling Esmeralda at the moment, so she's going to be late."

"Do you know how long they'll be with her?"

"They talked to me for a good half an hour," Samantha said. "I tried to get her to come with me, but the angels said they couldn't postpone their questioning and shut the door in my face."

"We'll start without her," I said. "Everybody else is inside." I led Samantha into the kitchen. She greeted Lila and Auntie Queenie before sitting at the table.

I'd also collected Wiggles from my apartment, and he sat next to Auntie Queenie, begging for treats.

I settled in a seat, and Auntie Queenie nodded at me to begin. I looked around the table at the anxious faces. "We have a new theory about why members of the gang are dying."

"What is it?" Samantha asked as she accepted a cup of tea from Auntie Queenie.

"Give Tempest a minute, and she'll tell you," Auntie Queenie said.

"We think it's somebody from your past. Someone whose magic was given to you to test on behalf of the Magic Council. Whoever it is, they've come back for revenge."

Auntie Queenie, Samantha, and Lila all talked at once, disputing, throwing out names, suggesting spells used. I gave them a minute before gesturing for silence.

"I know it's been a long time since you've had anything to do with testing magic for the Council, but I think it's relevant."

"How do you even know about that?" Samantha asked.

"Because she's nosy." Auntie Queenie winked at me. "And it's a good thing she is. Tempest found the record book I keep."

"I only found it because you left it on the kitchen table," I said. "You can't deal with this on your own. Two of you have already been killed, and Lila is sick. You need help."

Samantha nodded. "You know we can't talk about specifics of the magic we tested."

"I've had an idea about how to get around that," Auntie Queenie said. "We use replacement words for the spells. I know, for example, if I talk about this particular spell," she tapped a page on the book before passing it around the table, "I won't be able to utter a word. What if I called it the Spell of Orange?"

"It should work," Lila said. "I'm not sure how useful it will be, though."

"If it helps you all to talk it out, then try that. You need to come up with a shortlist of the most powerful magic from that book," I said. "Whoever's power you took is after you."

"Do you really think they'd wait this long to get back at us?" Samantha looked doubtful.

"There must be a reason they've waited this long. Maybe they've only just learned about your involvement with the Magic Council. But whatever the reason, they're here, and they want you all dead."

"I've marked the spells with that traffic light signal you saw in the book, Tempest. The green, amber, and red marks. We'll focus on the red ones. They were lethal, dark, and dangerous. That sort of magic should never be allowed to manifest. There were only twenty or so of those in the whole time we assisted the Magic Council."

I nodded. "Great, you go through those spells, and I'll sort out some food."

"Cake," Wiggles said. "It's essential in times of crisis."

"Your mom made a lovely buttercream sponge," Auntie Queenie said. "It's in the pantry."

I collected the cake and plates as Auntie Queenie, Samantha, and Lila huddled around the book, muttering to themselves and flicking through the pages as they read through the spells.

I busied myself with making more tea and cutting the cake as I tried not to worry. This was serious and deadly. We had to find out who was after them before the killer made their next move.

I'd never say it to them, but they were all vulnerable. Auntie Queenie had power, especially when it came to containing demons, but if what she said was true, and I had no reason to doubt it wasn't, the magic in that book was even stronger.

I set the fresh pot of tea and the sliced cake on the table before breaking off a few pieces and feeding them to Wiggles. "What have you got?"

"There are only three detailed in here that cause us concern," Auntie Queenie said. "There's the St…" her voice cut off, and she blinked rapidly.

"Give the magic another name," Lila said. "How about the Shoe of Banana? Yes! Listen, I can say Shoe of Banana, Shoe of Banana, Shoe of Banana as much as I like, and the restriction magic doesn't kick in."

I scratched my head. "The Shoe of Banana is meaningless to me."

"I'll show you the information in the book, but I used initials and shorthand for each item, so they couldn't be used or found if the book fell into the wrong hands," Auntie Queenie said. "Let's call this magic the Shoe of Banana for now, and you study my scribblings as I tell you about it."

She passed me the book and pointed at a line. The initials were S and B.

"Let's see how much we can reveal." Auntie Queenie cracked her knuckles. "The side effects of using this piece of magic were madness and death. It had the ability to turn an individual into stone."

"The Shoe of Banana must have belonged to a High Witch," I said.

Auntie Queenie nodded. "Owning the Banana wasn't a problem, providing you never used its full power."

"That's right," Lila said. "The Shoe of Banana had different levels of influence. For example, it could freeze someone to the spot for a moment before releasing them. That was considered permissible use."

"But the witch who had the Banana," Samantha said, "Agat…" her words faded.

"We can't say her name," Lila said.

"That's no good," I said. "How can I look out for a killer if you can't tell me who she is?"

"We'll have to make up a name for her," Samantha said.

"Grumpy Old Bird Face." Auntie Queenie grinned at the others. "She had a sharp nose and an even sharper tongue. She was always complaining about something."

Lila shrugged. "Mean but true. She did look like an old eagle whose favorite nesting site had been squashed."

"So, Grumpy Old Bird Face broke the rules," Auntie Queenie said. "She used the Banana's full power and killed people. A dozen people died before the Magic Council figured out what she was up to. They imprisoned her, took the Shoe of Banana away, and gave it to us."

"What did you do with it?" I asked.

"Drained it of its power," Samantha said. "It wasn't easy, and it was dangerous magic to tinker with. There was every possibility the Banana would explode and turn us all to stone."

"It was a close call. When we finally figured out how to deal with the magic, it was unstable. Banana splattered everywhere," Auntie Queenie said.

I wasn't sure what the banana was in this context, but I got the idea. The magic had been messy, and they'd almost died.

"It took three weeks to drain the Shoe of Banana's power," Samantha said. "After that, it was easy enough to destroy. Grumpy Old Bird Face wasn't happy when she learned what we'd done. I hear she still spits curses whenever anyone mentions us."

"If she's in prison, she's no danger to you," I said.

"That's just it. She's not," Auntie Queenie said. "Grumpy Old Bird Face vanished from prison almost a year ago. I remember thinking I needed to watch my back when I heard about her escape. After a while, when she didn't come looking for me, I figured she was too jaded and worn out to chase us after such a long time."

"And Grumpy Old Bird Face never focused her magic around fire. She always used stones and precious gems as a source of power. I'd be surprised if she's turned to fire," Lila said.

"She could have learned new skills while inside," Samantha said.

"Or she used fire as a diversion," Auntie Queenie said. "No one would think of Grumpy Old Bird Face using fire to kill."

I studied the scribbles and shorthand that referred to the Shoe of Banana. It was possible that this magic user had come back for revenge after losing something with so much power.

"Another dark piece of magic we've considered is the Book of..." Auntie Queenie's voice faded again. She sighed and shook her head.

"Don't use banana this time," I said.

"The Book of... Pumpkin," Auntie Queenie said. "Yes! A nasty little book full of curses. It was compiled by a twisted, spiteful, cold-hearted warlock."

"Let me name him!" Samantha clapped her hands together. "I never liked him. He always leered at my chest. He's called… Floppy Chops McFlappy Jowls."

Auntie Queenie and Lila chortled with laughter.

"That's a perfect description." Lila wiped a tear from the corner of her eye. "He looks like a Basset Hound in a wind tunnel."

I tipped my head back. For mature women, they sure had an interesting sense of humor. "What did Mister McFlappy Jowls do with this book?"

Auntie Queenie's smile faded. "Every page had the potential to kill."

"Floppy Chops McFlappy Jowls was building up to something big," Samantha said. "He'd collected these curses over a decade. He was never a popular guy and took offense easily. Alongside the Book of Pumpkin, there was a list of a hundred names. They were his targets. He'd planned an epic mission to kill everyone on his list using the curses in his nasty book."

"He almost got away with it," Auntie Queenie said. "He killed ten people before he was caught. The Magic Council took the book from him, sent him away for a long stretch, and ordered us to destroy his work."

"That was a horror to get rid of," Lila said. "We had to deal with each page individually and chant over it for twenty-four hours to leech the magic. There were one hundred curses."

"Where's Mister McFlappy Jowls now?" I asked.

"The last I heard about him," Auntie Queenie said, "he was still inside. He must be ancient by now, but he'd still be mean enough to hold a grudge against us. He knew we were involved with taking his magic. If he's gotten out without us realizing or been given an early release, I wouldn't put it past him to come here for revenge."

"So, we have Grumpy Old Bird Face and Floppy Chops McFlappy Jowls," I said. "One who likes earth magic and the other who favors curses. Neither of which were used on Bastille or Caprice. What's the final piece of magic?"

"It's a potion," Lila said, "the one the Magic Council gave us to destroy."

"The one that made everybody sick," Auntie Queenie said.

"Who did the Magic Council say the potion belonged to?" I asked.

"Baby Big Mouth." Lila grinned. "This magic user has a big round face and can never keep a secret. I called her Baby Cakes behind her back because I always wanted to squeeze those chubby cheeks."

"What magic does Baby Big Mouth specialize in?"

"She was a dark one," Auntie Queenie said. "She's supposed to have made this potion to kill her entire family. She was lost to dark magic and had become convinced her family hated her and was trying to kill her."

"Did she have any reason to believe that was true?"

"None at all. You know her family. They're the…" Auntie Queenie's words died. "Anyway, you know them. They wouldn't harm another family member. Baby Big Mouth wasn't strong enough to handle the dark magic she'd gotten lost in. She created this twisted, poisonous potion that acted slowly. If a person drank it or got it on their skin, it ate away at their health. It made them sick over several years, draining them of joy and happiness."

My eyebrows rose slowly. "That's the potion that exploded all over the gang?"

Auntie Queenie nodded, her expression glum. "Everyone was weakened. When I returned to find the gang in such disarray, I thought I'd lose them all."

"Queenie was incredible." Samantha patted Auntie Queenie's arm. "She used every magic trick she knew to get us on the mend. She brought in professionals, called in all of her favors, and didn't leave our sides until we were recovered."

"You'd have done the same for me." Auntie Queenie smiled at Samantha. "But it wasn't enough. Not for everybody."

I looked carefully at Samantha. Although she had some color in her cheeks, there was still tiredness under her eyes. "You were there?"

"Oh, yes." Samantha shifted in her seat. "I've been doing well for years. The potion didn't seem to bother me. But, as I'm getting older, I feel the dark magic gnawing at my bones. I've tried everything to dislodge it. My time is coming to an end."

"Nonsense," Auntie Queenie said. "You're a vivacious and beautiful woman."

Samantha shook her head. "It takes a lot of effort to be this vivacious. I like to think I'm still young and as full of energy as I was thirty years ago, but it's not true. I use most of my magical energy to maintain myself. I can't do it much longer. As great as your tonics are, Queenie, this magic is beating me. Just as it was beating Bastille."

"Was Caprice also getting weak because of this potion?" I asked.

"She fared better than Bastille," Auntie Queenie said. "Bastille got at least half of the potion on her. She swallowed some as well, which is never good."

"The rest of us got splashed with it," Samantha said.

"You're a strong witch. You'll beat this." Sadness clouded Auntie Queenie's vision. "I'm not losing any more of my gang."

Samantha smiled sadly and patted her hand.

I blinked tears out of my eyes and let my hair fall over my face as I pretended to study the book. It wasn't fair what had happened. Auntie's gang had been helping the Magic Council. They'd gotten re-paid by having a deadly potion inflicted on them.

Auntie Queenie's hand settled on my knee, and she gave it a gentle squeeze. "We've still got fire in our bellies. And having you here to sort this out is just what we need."

I cleared my throat and nodded. I'd solve this. If they were all sick, the last thing they needed was some sleazy, dark magic using maniac after them.

"We've got three possible attackers," I said. "But I don't know any of their names."

"Our descriptive names should help," Lila said. "Look for a grumpy old eagle, a guy with floppy jowls, and a woman with a moon face who never stops gossiping."

I shut the book and slid it onto the center of the table. I knew most people in Willow Tree Falls, so finding any of these unusual looking strangers wouldn't be tricky.

Auntie Queenie touched the book. "We did it because we thought we were helping the Magic Council."

"We also did it because we were full of ourselves," Lila said. "We know how powerful we are, and when we joined forces, we were almost unstoppable. We got arrogant."

"We have a right to be," Auntie Queenie said. "Our joined power is incredible. It's just a shame the Magic Council came to see us as a threat as opposed to an ally."

"Do you really think the Magic Council wants you dead?" I asked. "I can take on three dodgy magic users, but the entire Council? Even Frank would struggle with that."

"No," Lila said. "It's not the Council. They're the good guys."

"Maybe it's them." Auntie Queenie sank back in her seat. "But we should look at these three suspects first. As you said, they're a manageable problem. Taking down an ancient, powerful magic body, not so much."

"You all need to be in a safe house," I said. "Lila and Samantha, you can't go back to the hotel. The killer found Bastille and Caprice there. Staying on your own puts you at risk."

"You can stay here," Auntie Queenie said. "There's safety in numbers, and we've got the room."

I glanced at the kitchen door. "I thought Esmeralda would be finished with the angels by now."

"You're right," Samantha said. "They can't have been quizzing her for this long."

A shiver of worry ran through me. I hoped she wasn't about to be victim number three. "You all stay here. And stay together. Don't separate, not even to use the bathroom."

"McFlappy Jowls won't be hiding behind the shower curtain," Auntie Queenie said.

"Even so, no one stays on their own. If you're together, you're stronger." I pushed back my chair and stood. "I'll get Esmeralda and bring her here."

As I left the house with Wiggles, unease shifted through me. What if Auntie Queenie's concerns were justified, and it wasn't any of the magic users in her book? You don't go up against the Magic Council and win.

I had no idea how I'd stop everyone in the gang dying if it was the Council chasing them, but I was determined to try.

I wasn't losing another one of these witches, no matter who was hunting them.

Chapter 19

"I have a bad feeling about this," Wiggles said as we walked away from Mom's house. "We know about powerful magic, but this is hardcore."

"Tell me about it," I said. "I can't go to the Magic Council and petition to stop them from killing Auntie Queenie and her friends."

"You could, but it would take a dozen meetings and six fifty-page forms filled in before they'd even agree to meet you. They're suit wearing, stuffy pencil pushers who don't get their hands dirty."

"Which means, if the Magic Council is involved, they've hired a freelancer. Someone with lethal skills."

"Someone just like Auntie Queenie and her gang," Wiggles said.

I nodded as we reached the hotel and walked into the reception.

The reception desk was empty, so I hurried up the stairs and knocked on Esmeralda's door. It pushed open as I leaned against it. "Esmeralda, it's Tempest."

There was no reply. I walked into the bedroom to find it empty.

"She's left half a cookie." Wiggles hurried over and scoffed the cookie sitting on the edge of the dressing table.

I walked to the table and lifted the mug by the cookie crumbs. The contents were warm. "She hasn't been gone long. She could have ducked into a store on her way to Mom's house and we missed her."

"What's this?" Wiggles bounced on the bed. He had a piece of paper between his teeth.

I took the paper and read it. "Let's meet at the stone circle at twelve-thirty to discuss the offer." I turned it over. There was no name on the note, but it must have been for Esmeralda.

"What offer? Who's she going to meet?" Wiggles asked.

"I don't know, but I don't like this. If Esmeralda's on her own, it makes her vulnerable. Why would the angels leave her alone when there's a killer on the loose?"

"The angels know nothing about the Magic Council's involvement or the dodgy characters from Queenie's book," Wiggles said. "Esmeralda's a clever witch. She won't meet some weirdo who left an elusive note on her bed, not with everything that's going on."

"So, she must know the person who sent her this message." I hurried back down the stairs with Wiggles. A quick check of the garden and dining room confirmed Esmeralda wasn't in the hotel.

We left and hurried up the hill toward the stone circle.

I was almost running as we reached the top of the hill and sucked in a breath as I looked around.

"I hear voices coming from the circle," Wiggles said.

"Keep to the edge of the tree line. Let's see who Esmeralda's meeting." We inched closer to the stone circle, using the dense shadows of the forest to hide our movements.

I ducked as I spotted Esmeralda. She stood just inside the stone circle with her back to us.

Standing opposite her was a tall, broad-shouldered man with slicked-back dark hair wearing a gray suit and a neat black tie.

"He looks official," Wiggles muttered. "I'm getting the definite whiff of Magic Council."

"Me too," I whispered. "But why is Esmeralda meeting him here?" I gestured Wiggles to follow me and crept closer until we could hear their voices clearly.

I ducked behind a bush with Wiggles and settled in to hear what they were talking about.

"It's not good enough," Esmeralda said, her tone suggesting she was deeply unhappy.

"It's the best you'll get." The man's voice was high-pitched and petulant. "You can complain all you like, but it's a generous settlement."

I glanced at Wiggles and shrugged. "What settlement?"

"No! It has to be an individual settlement. You've tricked me. What you're offering is unfair."

The man's expression hardened. "It's only unfair to everybody else involved. We're the ones being honest, here."

"Honest! You wouldn't know what that word meant if it leaped off one of these stones and kicked you in the behind." Esmeralda paced in front of him. "I put in the effort. I made the claim as an individual. You're twisting things."

"By making that claim, you implicated others." The man looked at the papers in his hand. "You stated that you weren't the only one affected."

"To show I'm not making this up. No one else is interested in compensation."

"The group settlement stands." The man lowered the papers. "You take that offer, or you go away and stop bothering us."

"A group claim for compensation?" My brow wrinkled. It sounded like Esmeralda was chasing the Magic Council for money. But money for what?

"If you make that offer just to me, I'll accept it immediately." Esmeralda jabbed a finger. "I'll sign on the line right now, and you won't hear from me again."

The guy in the suit snorted a laugh. "You'd love that. There's enough money in this group settlement to set you up for the rest of your miserable life."

"And it will be miserable. I'm suffering. I feel sick every day, and my memory is fading. That's your fault."

I sucked in a breath, and my heart raced. "This is about the potion that misfired. Esmeralda's suffering because of it, too."

"And she's chasing the Magic Council for compensation," Wiggles said.

The man crossed his arms over his chest. "The Magic Council agreed to an out of court settlement with the entire group. Split the money between all of you and the problem is solved. You'll have a cozy retirement somewhere quiet. A nurse can dose you up with calming magic and sedatives until you give up the ghost and stop bothering us. But that's all you're getting."

Esmeralda scowled at him. "I deserve more. I led this claim. You settle only with me. I never mentioned a group settlement."

"Esmeralda's gotten greedy," Wiggles whispered.

I shook my head. It sounded like it, but I couldn't believe she'd be so merciless. Auntie Queenie and the gang were Esmeralda's oldest friends. They'd been through so much together. Would she turn on them to get her hands on this money?

The man smirked. "If you go down this road and insist on all the money, we'll ruin you. We'll tie this matter up in court with nit-picking questions and legal loopholes. You'll be poor and too sick to care by the time we've finished with you. Any money you get from us will be eaten up in legal fees. And when you lose, you'll pay all our costs, as well. Take the group offer. It's the easy way out."

"For you," she said. "When that money is split between us, it'll barely cover my upcoming medical bills. I've booked a month with a voodoo shaman in Haiti and an immersive healing cleanse with the demi-goddess Panacea."

"You have expensive tastes."

"I'll try anything to get better. Bastille was drowning in debt because she was so desperate to get well. The offer you're making wouldn't have helped her."

The man shrugged. "Bastille could have paid off her debts and had a little left over to pay for her funeral."

"That's my point!" Esmeralda was almost yelling. "If she'd lived, she'd have had no quality of life. Bastille couldn't have kept trying different spells and ways to heal herself. She was borrowing money to get by as it was."

"Even if she'd had all the money in the world, it would have been wasted. There's no cure," the man said. "We have records of that potion. We know where it came from and what its purpose was. Once you've been contaminated, you don't get better. You fade. You're fading, Esmeralda. Why use your last years fighting something you'll never win?"

I shifted my position to stop my feet from going to sleep. My emotions were torn. I understood why Esmeralda was suing the Magic Council, but why keep it a secret from the others? If they worked together, they could get the Council on the ropes and squeeze more out of them.

My hand flew to my mouth as a dark, horrible idea entered my head. "No, she wouldn't."

Wiggles cocked his head. "What are you thinking?"

I swallowed, my stomach clenching. "The Magic Council has offered compensation to everyone made sick by the exploding potion."

Wiggles nodded. "That sounds right."

My breath came out shaky, my brain rejecting the idea every time I jumped on it. "Esmeralda doesn't want a group settlement because it means she'll get less money."

He nodded again.

"Wiggles, think about it. The fewer people left alive in the group contaminated by the potion, the more money there will be for each of them."

Wiggles closed his eyes for a second before a growl slid from his mouth. "Esmeralda's killing everyone until she's the only one left."

"Which means, she'll get all the money."

"She'll have to kill Lila, Samantha—"

"And Auntie Queenie." My hands balled into fists. Esmeralda wasn't one of the gang. She was an enemy.

"What's it going to be, Esmeralda?" the man asked. "Let's end this nonsense now. Take the deal. Share the love with your old cronies."

"You can stuff your deal," Esmeralda said. "I'll get all that money, one way or the other."

"Then I'll see you in court."

My eyes widened as fire flared on Esmeralda's hands.

The guy in the suit laughed as he clicked his fingers and vanished.

Esmeralda screamed and shot a ball of fire into the air.

"That is one unstable lady," Wiggles whispered.

I nodded. "She's sick and greedy. She'll do anything to get her hands on that money."

"Even killing her oldest friends," Wiggles growled. "I need to bite her."

Frank stirred inside me. "Having problems with a greedy, old witch?"

"Something like that," I muttered.

"I always enjoy teaching witches a lesson," Frank said. "If you'd like me to play with her, I've nothing better on this afternoon."

I was tempted to let Frank go to town on Esmeralda. It was no less than she deserved. "Let's see what she has to say before you have your fun."

"Be careful," Wiggles said. "She's already killed two people, people she was supposed to care about. When Esmeralda finds out that you know what she's been up to, she won't hesitate getting rid of you."

It hurt to hear that, but it was the truth. Maybe the sickness had stopped her from thinking clearly, but Esmeralda had to be stopped.

"We'll see about that." I stood and was about to confront Esmeralda when a figure dressed in black darted from behind a stone. They threw themselves at Esmeralda, taking her to the ground.

My eyes widened as I stared at this unexpected arrival.

Esmeralda shrieked and rolled over as the black-clad attacker shot magic at her.

I shook my head. What was going on?

"Whoever jumped Esmeralda knows how to fight." Wiggles winced as a blast of gray light pinged off Esmeralda and made the surrounding colors fade and the air cold.

"Come on. We need answers from Esmeralda before this stranger kills her. We have to stop this."

Chapter 20

Esmeralda shrieked and hurled a spell at her attacker as we hurried closer to the standing stones.

I slowed, my eyes wide as I watched Esmeralda fight this stranger. Her attacker was tall and slim, and from the fit of her ninja-style clothing, looked female. Whoever it was, they were fast, strong, and using magic with lethal abandon.

"Have we made a mistake?" I asked Wiggles.

"I never make a mistake."

"I mean, we thought Esmeralda was the killer." I flinched as a bolt of jagged red magic flickered around the stone circle. "Maybe we got it wrong. This is the killer, and she's after Esmeralda."

The ninja attacker was blasted off her feet but spun in the air and landed in a crouched position, her hand extended, ready with more attack magic.

"You're not getting rid of me that easily," Esmeralda screamed. She blasted another spell.

Her attacker threw up her arms, and the magic bounced away before striking.

"This can't be any of the magic users Auntie Queenie and the others identified. They'd be ancient by now and not capable of moving like that ninja."

Esmeralda raced toward the attacker, her hands flaming. She grabbed her as she dodged away and wrapped her hands around her neck.

"Look! That's how Caprice and Bastille were killed." I stepped closer as I watched Esmeralda strangle her attacker, her fingers blazing white hot.

The black-clad attacker wrestled with Esmeralda before blasting her in the chest with a spell and sending her flying. She smacked against the side of a standing stone and fell to the ground.

The ninja stalked toward her, flickers of green magic sparking on her fingers.

I edged closer with Wiggles, keeping an eye on the attacker. I couldn't let Esmeralda die. I was still uncertain if she was innocent or guilty, and she had a lot of questions to answer.

Esmeralda tried to get to her feet but staggered and fell. She held her hand against one side, and her face was pale. Still, she was a fighter, and flames flickered on her hand as she held it out to ward off her attacker.

The ninja stood over Esmeralda and raised her hands.

"That's enough!" I stepped out from behind a stone and entered the circle.

The attacker wheeled and crouched.

"Oh! Tempest! You have to help me." Esmeralda struggled onto her knees. "This is the person who murdered the others. She's trying to kill me."

The attacker didn't move, but her attention remained on me. "This isn't your business. Leave now."

"I'm going nowhere," I said. "Why are you attacking Esmeralda?"

"I've told you," Esmeralda spluttered. "This is the person you want. She murdered Bastille and Caprice."

The attacker's head tilted. She wore a black fitted face mask, so I had no idea who she was. "I'm here to kill one person. Esmeralda DuPont."

"Why?" I inched closer and felt Frank's energy spiral up my spine as he felt the power of the mystery woman.

"Be careful of this one," Frank cautioned. "She has a higher authority backing her."

"How do you know?" I whispered.

"It's my job to know trouble when I see it."

"Help me!" Esmeralda said. "I can't fight her on my own. Between us, we can take her down. This is who we've been searching for. We have to bring her to justice. For Bastille and Caprice."

"I'm here to administer justice today, not you." The attacker turned and blasted Esmeralda onto her back.

I sparked my own magic. Being in the center of the stone circle enhanced my power. The stones were ancient and full of magic. They'd seen thousands of years of supernatural activity. They absorbed it and held onto traces of power.

I touched a stone and felt a satisfying throb of energy before blasting out a bolt of green light and knocking the attacker off her feet.

She bounced up like she was made of rubber and raced toward me, blasting spells that weren't meant to miss.

I dodged several but was spun off my feet when one caught me in the side.

I gritted my teeth as a hot, jagged lance of pain ripped through me. This assassin wasn't playing fair. Her magic had a gray tinge, suggesting she had experience with darker powers.

I dodged around a stone and dragged in air. Wiggles sat looking up at me.

"Any time you want to blast the attacker with fire, you're most welcome," I gasped.

"That happens on special occasions and is rarely under my control," Wiggles said. "You've got this."

My eyebrows rose. I wasn't so sure. This assassin's magic was strong. She also wasn't a demon, and that was where my speciality lie.

I glanced around the stone to see the ninja attacker turn back to Esmeralda. She must have thought she'd scared me off, but I wasn't done yet.

I ducked out from behind the stone and blasted her in the back with a swirl of magic zapping energy. She staggered forward but remained upright as she pivoted toward me.

"That's not good," Wiggles muttered as he peered around the stone. "It's like she barely felt that spell."

"Get back." I nudged Wiggles to safety just before I was flung backwards and pinned against a stone. My arms and legs were splayed, and I couldn't move, no matter how much I struggled. The binding magic slid over my body like rancid, sticky tar.

The ninja attacker glided toward me like she was walking on air. "Stay out of this. This isn't your business. I don't want to kill you, but I will if you keep getting in my way."

"Why are you here?" I struggled against the power in her binding spell. "If you're only here to kill Esmeralda, why kill the others?"

The assassin glanced back to where Esmeralda was slumped. "I've killed many times, but this time, my assignment is the death of one witch. If other murders have taken place here, they've not been by my hand."

I glared at her. "Why should I believe you?"

"I'm paid per kill. I don't do freebies. Now, sit back and enjoy the show." She patted my cheek before turning and striding toward Esmeralda.

I wasn't sure who to believe, but the assassin sounded certain. She had a job to do and was here to carry it out. There was also no reason she'd lie to me. Someone had sent her here to kill Esmeralda. This all came back to the money Esmeralda was trying to get out of the Magic Council.

I struggled to get free, but the spell held. "Wiggles, how are you doing?"

He poked his head around the stone, his red eyes glowing with excitement. "Don't worry about me. All

I need is popcorn and this will make for great entertainment."

"This isn't for your entertainment. I could die."

"Do you want me to take on the assassin?" He moved closer and growled.

"No! She's too strong. We need reinforcements."

"I can run back to the house and get help."

"We don't have time for that."

"What do you need?"

I gritted my teeth. I needed Frank. His extra energy could break this spell. "Don't get too close. Frank's coming out." I let down my barriers and encouraged his power to fill me.

He wasted no time sliding up my spine and over my head. As he took over, I felt his lust for a fight.

My body grew uncomfortably warm then agonizingly hot from the inside as his powers burned away the spell trapping me against the stone.

I dropped to the ground with a gasp, sweat running down my back as Frank gained complete control and the world took on a red tinted glow.

"Who shall we deal with first?" Frank asked.

"I have to talk to Esmeralda," I said, my own voice echoing in my head. "Keep her alive."

"And the assassin?"

"Is just that, an assassin. A hired killer. She must know the risks of such a profession."

Frank laughed. "Tempest Crypt, you're giving me permission to kill?"

A big part of me wanted to say yes, but I was intrigued by this mystery woman. Who hired her to come after Esmeralda? "Keep her alive."

"I promise nothing," Frank said. "Let's go dance with danger."

He was always so dramatic. I headed toward Esmeralda and the assassin, Frank's power bubbling through me.

She turned and shook her head. "You don't know when to quit."

"I could say the same for you." My voice sounded deeper when Frank was in charge.

The assassin's head tilted. "You're different."

"And you're dead." A dark, sticky power shot from me and blasted the assassin onto her back.

It took a few seconds before she struggled back on her feet. Frank's power always had a nasty sting to it. She shook her head and backed away. "What are you?"

"Your executioner."

"Easy now," I said to Frank. "We need her to talk."

I felt Frank's excitement curl through me. He always enjoyed a good throw down fight. "Who sent you to kill Esmeralda?"

"I never talk about my clients." The assassin continued to back up, her knees bent and arm splayed. Magic sparked on the tips of her fingers, but she didn't throw anything at me.

"You don't like to talk, but I love to make people confess their sins." I dodged from side to side as Frank tried to spook the assassin with fast, jerky movements.

"The vibe you're giving off is unnatural."

"I take that as a compliment," Frank said. "Why don't I show you how unnatural I am?" He lunged me through the air, and I wrapped an arm around the assassin's neck.

She flipped me over her head, and I rolled out of the way as a spell slammed into the ground an inch from my ear.

I shook my head, trying to dislodge the loud ringing sound.

The assassin threw several spells, one after the other. I dodged, jumped, and weaved in an unnaturally fast pattern, thanks to Frank's flood of power and control over my movements.

"Take her down," I muttered to Frank. "You're playing with her and me."

"I like to play," he said. "You don't let me out often enough."

A stream of black energy flew from me and wrapped around the assassin's neck like a lasso. I hauled her toward me as she tried to burn through Frank's energy with her own magic.

But Frank was an ancient demon. His ability was strong and dark and not easy to conquer.

The assassin sank to her knees, choking as her hands fell to her sides.

I approached and stared down at her. "Frank, let me talk to her."

"I'll handle her." He forced my arm to move and yanked the mask off her head.

The woman revealed was in her thirties, with pale blue eyes and cropped blonde hair. She glared up at me, her breath gasping out as Frank's energy continued to drain her.

"Who are you?"

She shook her head. "That's not important. I'm here to do a job, that's all."

"Who hired you to do this job?"

The assassin looked away. "I don't remember their name."

I knelt until I was eye level and growled in her face. "As you noticed, there's something wonderfully unnatural about me. On the outside, I look like some cute little witch, but there's more going on than you realize. You're lucky I don't twist your head from your scrawny neck."

"No removing of heads," I whispered to Frank.

He grunted in response. "Tell me who you work for and why they hired you to kill Esmeralda."

The assassin grimaced but didn't say a word.

"Speaking of Esmeralda," Wiggles shouted from his spot behind the stones, "she's making a run for it."

I jumped up and looked around the stone circle.

Esmeralda was running toward the trees. Once she got into the forest, she'd be impossible to find.

"Hellhound, get after her. Don't let Esmeralda go."

Wiggles' legs were a blur as he raced after Esmeralda, who limped as she ran and still clutched her side. He reached her and grabbed the back of her skirt in his mouth.

Esmeralda shrieked but kept running, dragging Wiggles behind her as he dug his paws into the ground and held on tight.

Frank moved me away from the assassin. He raised my hand, and a black ball of what looked like sticky mud shot toward Esmeralda.

It slammed into the back of her head, and she face-planted into the ground.

Wiggles flew over the top of her and rolled across the ground. He jumped up, shook out his fur, and glared at me. "I was on top of things."

"My apologies, my little hellhound."

"You owe me for that, Frank," Wiggles grumbled. He turned to face Esmeralda and growled at her, but she was going nowhere. She was stuck to the ground and covered in a toxic looking mud.

I walked over and flipped Esmeralda onto her back. She lay there blinking at me. "Why did you attack me? I'm the innocent party."

"You were running. Only the guilty run." Frank wasn't gentle as he laced my fingers around her ankle and pulled her back into the stone circle.

The assassin was crawling away on her hands and knees. A quick warning blast of magic halted her slow escape.

"My turn, Frank." I had to be in control of the questioning. His lust for blood was growing, and I couldn't have either of these women killed before all the questions were answered.

He growled in my head and pushed against me but slowly faded, and along with his energy, all the murderous thoughts he fed me vanished.

I dragged Esmeralda over to the assassin. "Start talking," I said to Esmeralda.

"This is who you should interrogate." She pointed a wavering finger at the mystery woman.

"You'll both get interrogated," I said. "I overheard you. You're trying to get money out of the Magic Council."

Esmeralda licked her lips. "I was making a deal for everyone."

"Everyone affected by the dodgy potion given to you by the Magic Council?"

Her mouth fell open before she snapped her jaw shut and sighed. "Queenie showed you the book."

"The group told me everything. Well, everything they could. I know about the potion."

She raised her chin. "We deserve fair compensation for what happened. The Magic Council is in the wrong. They have to pay."

"And they offered you a group settlement," I said. "Wasn't that enough?"

"It was more than enough."

"For you." Wiggles trotted over and sat by my heel. "So long as you don't have to share it."

Esmeralda glared at him. "That money is for everyone left in our group."

"How much are we talking about?" I asked.

"It's ten million," Esmeralda said.

My eyebrows shot up. "Ten million each?"

"No, between all surviving members of the group. Anyone who had direct contact with the potion will receive a share of the money."

"Notice she said *surviving* members," Wiggles muttered.

I nodded. "Which means, the fewer members in the group, the more money you'll get. That's why you killed Caprice and Bastille."

Esmeralda refused to meet my gaze. "They're my friends."

It didn't sit well with me that Esmeralda was the killer, but the evidence was overwhelming. "Are you having money problems? Is that why you did this?"

"Of course not! I intended to take what I'm entitled to."

The assassin snorted.

"Have you got something to say?" I asked her. "Who are you? I can't keep thinking of you as the assassin."

"My name's not important. Besides, that's an accurate description of what I do."

"Your name will be important when I hand you over to the angels for attempted murder," I said.

She shrugged. "They can't hold me."

"Let's call her Daisy," Wiggles said. "She looks like a Daisy. Sort of cute and harmless."

"You mangy mutt. I'm not called Daisy. I'm—" she snarled at Wiggles and looked away.

"You see, cute as a button," Wiggles said.

"Fine, I'm Daisy. Whatever you like," the assassin, now known as Daisy, muttered.

I shrugged. It was as good a name as any. "Okay, Daisy. What do you know about these murders?"

"I'm only interested in Esmeralda. She's my target. That's who I've been watching since I arrived in

Willow Tree Falls yesterday. I just needed an opportunity to get Esmeralda on her own."

"Who hired you?"

"I don't recall."

"The Magic Council?"

Daisy snorted. "Who knows?"

"You do. It's too much of a coincidence that someone from the Magic Council arrives with a deal for Esmeralda, and when she doesn't take it, you appear, all magic blazing."

"You know what they say, life is full of coincidences."

I wasn't buying that. "Why did the Magic Council hire you?"

Daisy looked away. "It doesn't matter who hired me. The only thing I'm telling you is that I had nothing to do with these other murders. I got here yesterday. I'll be leaving today."

"Neither did I," Esmeralda said. "I'm innocent."

"You're not that innocent," I said. "I watched you use fire magic to strangle Daisy. That was how Bastille and Caprice were killed."

"In self-defense," Esmeralda said. "I'd have done anything to escape her. She's dangerous. Only when she's behind bars will the rest of us be safe."

"If you need my alibi, I have one," Daisy said. "I was doing… a bit of business in another part of the country. I have victims who, well, they can't talk anymore, but my particular style of dispatch is unique."

"Your style of dispatch?" I swallowed, feeling disgusted at how easily she talked about killing.

"We all have bills to pay."

"Get a job behind a bar," I said.

Daisy only smirked and toyed with a blade of grass.

My heart sank as I glared at Esmeralda. It wouldn't be hard to check Daisy's movements and confirm who she killed. Esmeralda was the killer. She'd murdered Bastille and Caprice to get her hands on their share of the pay out from the Magic Council.

I'd heard enough. It was time to bring in reinforcements. But before I got the angels involved, there were other people who'd want to speak to Esmeralda.

Chapter 21

Fifteen minutes later, I spotted Wiggles returning from Mom's house with Auntie Queenie, Samantha, and Lila.

"Tempest, what's going on?" Auntie Queenie hurried over, concern on her face. "Wiggles said you'd found the killer."

"I have." Esmeralda and Daisy sat with their backs against a stone in the circle. Esmeralda looked nervous, and Daisy appeared bored.

"Who's that?" Samantha pointed at Daisy. "I don't know her."

"Neither do I," I said. "She came out of the shadows and attacked Esmeralda."

"That's Bastille and Caprice's killer?" Lila advanced toward Daisy, her hands clenched.

I caught hold of Lila's arm. "Sadly not." I looked at Esmeralda. "Do you want to tell them?"

Esmeralda sighed and looked away. "I had no choice. And I deserve that money."

"What money?" Auntie Queenie asked. "What's going on?"

Esmeralda glanced at her friends before ducking her head. "I'm also sick. I've been fighting it for a while, but the potion is finally getting to me. Six months ago, I went to my doctor. He said there's not much more he can do. It's a case of time. I'll fade slowly over the next few years. I refuse to go out with a whimper. I know there's something out there that will help me."

"What's this got to do with our dead friends?" Samantha asked.

Esmeralda shifted on the ground. "I've been trying to get the Magic Council to accept responsibility for that potion they gave us. Once they do that, it's only right they offer compensation for what happened to us."

"Responsibility? Huh, I never thought about going after them for compensation," Auntie Queenie said.

"Neither did I. Not until I read about a case in a newsletter run by a Magic Council hater. She claimed the Magic Council uses their funds to keep magic users quiet when things go wrong. They paid a witch a huge sum of money because she'd experimented with a spell they gave her and had almost died."

"What spell did she use that was so deadly?" Lila asked.

"The spell isn't important," I said. "It's the money she got offered that Esmeralda is interested in."

Esmeralda nodded. "It had been hushed up, but I discovered the witch's name and got in touch with her. She told me how she winkled money out of the Magic Council. It wasn't difficult but needed time and lots of paperwork. I've been working on getting us compensation for almost a year."

"Since our last reunion?" Lila asked.

"You should have said," Auntie Queenie said. "We could have helped."

"Esmeralda didn't want help," I said. "Keep going. What did the Magic Council offer you?"

Esmeralda scowled at me before shaking her head. "They offered me a settlement, but when it was divided between us, it wouldn't have made any difference. I have plans for my last few years. There are new treatments I want to try, and I'd planned to spend a year sailing the world, eating fine foods, and drinking amazing wine. I want to make love under the stars on a Caribbean island with a gorgeous guy half my age."

Auntie Queenie snorted a laugh. "It's a lovely dream, but you're a bit old for that." She took a step closer to Esmeralda.

I caught hold of Auntie Queenie's arm. "Best not to get too close."

Auntie Queenie's brow wrinkled. "I didn't know you were so ill, Esmeralda."

"It was a shock to me, as well. It came on quickly."

"And the money you were offered?" I prodded her to continue. "What did you decide to do about the offer from the Magic Council?"

She glowered at me. "The Council wasn't budging. If I was to achieve half of what I wanted before I faded, I had to act fast."

"So, what did you do?" Samantha's anxious gaze shifted from Daisy to Esmeralda.

Esmeralda pinched her lips together and shook her head.

"Esmeralda killed Bastille and Caprice," I said.

Auntie Queenie gasped and grabbed Lila and Samantha's arms. "She wouldn't do such a thing. She's one of us."

I gestured for Esmeralda to continue, but she looked away and crossed her arms over her chest.

"Esmeralda was offered a group settlement by the Magic Council. Ten million divided between all surviving members. Anyone who'd been in contact with the jinxed potion was eligible for a payout. Esmeralda figured it wasn't enough when divided between you all. However, the fewer the number of gang members left, the bigger the payout would be."

Nobody spoke as this information sank in.

"Esmeralda planned to kill us off to get a bigger payout for herself?" Auntie Queenie's face paled.

"But we were drinking cocoa together when Bastille was killed," Lila said. "How could you be in two places at once?"

"Didn't you say you dozed off?" I asked her.

"Well, yes, I did struggle to keep my eyes open," Lila said. "I got really sleepy. When I woke, Esmeralda was tidying the mugs and about to leave."

I nodded. "And Esmeralda gave cocoa to Tabitha as well. She also fell asleep after drinking it." I glared at Esmeralda. "I wonder why that is?"

Esmeralda ducked her head. "A sleeping potion. I used it so I could get around without being noticed."

"You scheming old hag." Samantha advanced on Esmeralda.

Esmeralda cowered against Daisy, who shoved her away.

"I'm not getting involved with this," Daisy said. "If you were my friend and double-crossed me like that, I'd want to kill you too."

Esmeralda pressed her back against the stone. "Have mercy. I'm dying. Daisy beat me half to death."

"Who's Daisy?" Auntie Queenie looked confused.

Daisy tilted her chin. "Lethal killing machine at your service."

They stared at her in silence.

"Your niece is a menace, Queenie," Esmeralda said. "She let her demon loose on me. He stopped me from escaping."

Auntie Queenie sniffed. "I'm not a fan of Frank, but he did the right thing. You don't deserve to escape." She shook her head. "How could you kill Bastille and Caprice?"

"Bastille was almost dead, anyway," Esmeralda said, her expression growing cold. "We all saw how badly she suffered. In six months, she'd have been dead. Her share of the money would have vanished along with her if she'd received it. It would have been a waste."

"She could have enjoyed the time she had left," Samantha said. "You know how little money she had. Bastille could have taken a few holidays, treated herself, and taken her mind off her illness."

"But instead, you wanted it all for yourself," Lila snarled. "You're a heartless, evil witch."

"And greedy," Samantha said. "What about Caprice? She wasn't sick."

"I think she was," I said. "She was seen out of the hotel on the night of Bastille's murder. She didn't look too good."

Esmeralda nodded. "Caprice was in a bad way. She'd told me in confidence that she wasn't doing well. She'd visited a specialist in Norway and another in Canada to get second and third opinions. She'd been given some magic to ward off the worst of the symptoms, but she was going down almost as fast as Bastille. I figured she didn't have more than twelve months left."

"They were your friends." Auntie Queenie's magic sparkled out of her like a firework. "We were part of the same gang. We looked out for each other, no matter what. You attacked the weakest members of our group for personal greed. That cannot be forgiven."

"Who were you targeting next?" Samantha stood shoulder to shoulder with Auntie Queenie and Lila. "I've had symptoms recently, so has Lila. Which one of us were you planning to choke to death?"

Esmeralda had the decency to look away. "I needed that money. I wasn't going to spend my last months sitting in a moth-eaten armchair and cursing the Magic Council."

"By withholding that money from Caprice and Bastille, you took away any chance they had of a decent end." Auntie Queenie pulled back her shoulders. "We know the truth. It's time for justice."

"Finally!" Daisy stood. "If you want justice, that's why I'm here."

They all looked confused.

I raised a hand in warning. "Daisy was sent by a mysterious someone to kill Esmeralda."

Wiggles coughed out the words Magic Council.

Daisy shrugged. "I'm saying nothing about who sent me. This is what I'm here for. It sounds like you want this witch dead. Let me do my job, and I'll be on my way. I'd have been done by now if I hadn't been attacked by this… this creature." She gestured at me. "Whatever hybrid of magic creature you are, you're strong and damaged."

"Nonsense. My niece is perfect." Auntie Queenie patted my arm. "She has a little issue to deal with, that's all."

"She should be locked up. You must be able to feel her energy. You think Esmeralda's a danger, but she's the most unstable thing around here."

"Ignore her." Auntie Queenie's worried expression was masked by a smile. "She doesn't know you like we do."

I tried to ignore the shiver of worry inside me. I knew I had a problem with Frank, but I couldn't think about that now.

Lila scratched her head. "I'm confused. I got lost at the lethal assassin administering justice part?"

Daisy smirked. "You should have left me to complete my mission. Your problem would be gone."

"Your mission?" Lila asked.

"When I went to find Esmeralda, I discovered a note in her room telling her to come here," I said. "I overheard her talking to someone from the Magic Council about the group compensation offer. When he left, Daisy turned up."

"To kill me," Esmeralda said.

Auntie Queenie nodded. "Daisy's right. We should leave her to get on with it."

"That's a funny name for an assassin, Daisy," Lila said. "Is it a family name?"

Daisy sighed and pressed her lips together.

"Your greed made you a target," Samantha said to Esmeralda. "You brought this on yourself."

"You're a fine one to talk about money," Esmeralda said.

Samantha shrugged. "I earn mine."

"You mean, you married it," Esmeralda said.

"My husband's no walk in the park. He eats with his mouth open and never puts the loo seat down. Sometimes, I wonder if all that money is worth it."

I glanced at her, wondering if she was reconsidering her relationship status with Toby. Was Toby worth the trouble, or was he just another guy who ate with his mouth open and forgot the loo seat had a purpose.

Lila looked at Daisy. "Is this case still open?"

Daisy's brow wrinkled. "What do you mean?"

"I mean, the claim Esmeralda has against the Magic Council," Lila said. "If it's an active case, it sounds like we're entitled to our share of the money, so long as we're alive to claim it."

Esmeralda spluttered, and her cheeks turned puce. "You can't do that. It's taken me months to get to this stage. If the Magic Council hadn't tried to kill me, I'd have fixed a deal for us all. They were trying to scare me away with threats of lawsuits and bankruptcy, but I'd have gone after them."

"I doubt that. You'd have gone after the rest of your friends," I said. "You killed Bastille and Caprice, and I bet you had the rest of the gang in your sights."

Esmeralda glanced at Lila, Auntie Queenie, and Samantha. "I don't know what you're talking about."

"You mean old bag," Lila said. "Let's take our share of this money. Esmeralda's getting nothing. That's the perfect punishment for her. You can't spend your money when you're in prison."

Esmeralda groaned and pressed a hand to her injured side. "That's not fair."

"You lost the right to fairness after you killed our friends," Auntie Queenie said. "You deserve nothing."

"I deserve that money," Esmeralda said. "I worked hard for it."

"And two of our best friends lost their lives because of your hard work," Auntie Queenie said. "All you'll get is a long spell in prison." She looked over at me. "Have you informed the angels?"

I nodded at Wiggles. "Go round up some angels and get them here."

Wiggles grumbled before running off, muttering about the angels hating him and not letting him eat their doughnuts.

"What about Daisy?" Auntie Queenie asked. "How are we going to explain her?"

"You don't need to explain me," Daisy said. "I can look after myself."

"The angels will want to talk to you," I said. "You tried to kill Esmeralda."

"Prove it," Daisy said. "I'll say I was a concerned citizen who saw trouble and tried to help you take down a criminal."

"The angels won't need to do much digging to find a record on you. It sounds like this isn't your first time on the job," I said.

Daisy smirked. "Assuming you're right, and I work for the Magic Council, those kinds of records have a habit of disappearing."

"She's right," Auntie Queenie muttered. "The Magic Council is an officious bunch, but they've got a lethal side. As Esmeralda has discovered, if you cross them, you pay with your life."

"Which is what they tried to do to all of you," I said. "If they're responsible for that dodgy potion making you all sick, they won't want that information getting in the public domain."

"I wish I could prove it was them behind it," Auntie Queenie said. "It's time someone shook up that archaic system."

"The payment they're offering is a sort of proof," I said. "They feel responsible enough to give you money."

"It's hush money," Esmeralda said. "That's a part of the deal. I was taking this money but would have signed a waiver so I could never talk about it again. Ten million for my complete silence."

"So, no one will know how underhanded the Magic Council really is," I said. "That's clever of them."

"That's the Magic Council for you," Auntie Queenie said. "They like their dark deeds to remain hidden. What do you reckon girls? Do you fancy spending the rest of your days fighting the Magic Council to get them to admit they tried to bump us off?"

"There's not a chance I'm wasting the time I have left going after them," Samantha said. "I'd rather take the money and spend it on extravagant nonsense. Every time I sip a glass of champagne, I'll smile because I know I'm spending the Magic Council's money on something frivolous."

"I'm with Samantha," Lila said. "We'd waste what time we've got going to court, filing paperwork, and being hounded by the dubious tactics of the Magic Council. And, if we keep prodding them, what's to say they won't send another Daisy after us? If I'm going to die, I'm going out in style."

"That was my plan," Esmeralda whined. "You're stealing my plan and my money."

"You keep quiet," Auntie Queenie said, "or I'll let Tempest loose on you again."

I tilted my head and shrugged at Esmeralda. "You can't blame me for what happened. My demon has a mind of his own."

Frank chuckled inside my head. "And don't you forget it."

"We'll take the money." Auntie Queenie nudged Esmeralda with the toe of her shoe. "Don't expect any visits from us when you're inside. You're lucky we don't finish the job Tempest and Daisy started."

"But I'll die in prison," Esmeralda said. "I don't deserve that."

"And Bastille and Caprice didn't deserve to lose their lives," I said.

Esmeralda hung her head and sighed.

"I'm getting a toy boy," Lila said. "Someone who'll look after me and treat me like a goddess. He'll be skilled in the sensual art of Thai massage."

"A toy boy sounds exhausting," Samantha said. "How about a cruise? All expenses paid, food on tap, champagne whenever we want it. Dancing at night or seeing shows. Whatever we fancy."

"Will there be a masseuse on board?" Lila asked.

"Of course. You can hire one for your exclusive use. Some gorgeous guy can be on hand to give you a brisk rub down whenever you fancy."

"We should go on a year-long cruise." Auntie Queenie's eyes sparkled.

"I don't think Uncle Kenny can spare you for a whole year," I said.

She pursed her lips. "I would miss him if I was away for a whole year. We can start with three months. He'll enjoy a break from me. He always says I snore too loudly. He can catch up on his beauty sleep while we have an adventure at sea."

The women gathered together and continued talking about how they'd spend their windfall.

I shook my head and smiled as I listened to them. Something good had come out of this. The killer had been found, people I cared about who'd been mistreated by the Magic Council would get some comfort, and we knew what had happened to Caprice and Bastille.

My work was done. I'd have to look into having my own holiday. I needed it after this adventure.

Chapter 22

Three days had passed since Esmeralda's arrest for the murder of Caprice and Bastille. Willow Tree Falls felt back to normal.

I stood in the family cemetery with everyone. Lila and Samantha were also there, dressed in black, a red and white rose in each hand.

Two ornately carved, white marble plaques were on the ground in front of us. They commemorated the deaths of Caprice Gray and Bastille Drew.

Auntie Queenie wiped a tear from her cheek. "They were great girls."

"The best in the gang," Samantha said.

"Caprice always let me borrow her designer boots," Lila said. "She didn't even mind when I broke the heel on the last pair. She was so generous."

Mom patted Auntie Queenie's arm. "You girls had a great time together. Remember the good times.

Remember sharing fun and laughter and all the adventures you had."

"We did have amazing times," Auntie Queenie said. "I remember when Caprice stole a bike from a rival gang. She rode it around the village dressed in shiny red hot pants and a bikini top while they chased her. She kept throwing fireballs over her shoulder, not really caring what she hit. She rode through the barrier and out of Willow Tree Falls. She didn't come back for eight days. When she did, the bike had done over ten thousand miles. She said she'd just rode for hours, only stopping to refuel and hang out with cute guys."

"What about the time Bastille stole the gargoyle from outside the mayor's house?" Samantha said.

"Bastille did that?" My eyes widened. "She always seemed so sensible."

Auntie Queenie grinned. "Still waters run deep. She had a naughty side."

"That thing was heavy," Samantha said. "The gargoyle weighed more than I do. Someone challenged her that she'd never get the gargoyle without being seen."

"Bastille never said anything, didn't even confirm she'd accepted the challenge," Lila said. "But she had this sly smile, and you knew something devious was going on inside her head."

"I remember," Auntie Queenie said with a chuckle. "A week later, the gargoyle was gone and had been replaced by that hideous stuffed cat the mayor kept in his front window. The one with a missing eye and mangy fur."

Lila laughed. "The mayor was furious that someone broke into his house and stole his beloved stuffed cat. He didn't care about the gargoyle. All he wanted to know was who stole Fluffy."

"And where did the gargoyle magically reappear?" Auntie Queenie asked.

"In the mayor's toilet," Lila and Samantha said at the same time before laughing.

I smiled as I watched Auntie Queenie and her friends reminisce. They had lovely memories of their old friends. Bastille and Caprice would never be forgotten.

"Come on. I've got the food set up in the crypt," Mom said. "We can toast a farewell to Bastille and Caprice."

Auntie Queenie, Samantha, and Lila remained by the plaques as they placed their flowers and said their goodbyes, while the rest of us gave them privacy.

I wandered along next to Granny Dottie and Grandpa Lucius, looking forward to the feast Mom had prepared.

"I heard a rumor," Granny Dottie said, "about our mysterious assassin."

I slowed and looked at her. It was no secret that the angels had taken both Daisy and Esmeralda into custody when they'd arrived at the stone circle. "Do you know who she is?"

"No, she remains a mystery, and she'll continue to do so. I was getting coffee before coming here with your grandpa, and Brogan told me the assassin has vanished."

I grabbed her arm. "The angels let her go?" It would be just like them to make some blunder and release a paid assassin onto the streets.

"Oh no, they didn't let her go. She vanished. She was in a locked cell, and the next morning, there was no sign of her. The door was locked, and there was no window to get out of."

"The Magic Council," I hissed. "Daisy was so smug when she said there'd be no record of her."

Granny Dottie patted my hand. "It sounds like she was only interested in fulfilling her agreement with the Magic Council. Esmeralda's locked up and out of the way, so she's no longer considered a problem. And from what Brogan overheard from the angels, Esmeralda is raging about the Council trying to kill her. They think she's attempting to fake insanity, so she gets a lighter sentence. No one believes her."

I felt a slither of sympathy for Esmeralda. She was dying and had lost sight of what was important. She'd put her own temporary happiness in front of her friends. But she'd gotten what she deserved and would never get out of prison.

Granny Dottie glanced over my shoulder and winked at me. "I'll see you inside the crypt." She hurried away with Grandpa Lucius.

I turned and saw Rhett heading toward me, a smile on his face.

He placed a lingering kiss on my cheek. "I heard you were having a party."

"It's a sort of party. Auntie Queenie and her friends are remembering those they've lost. I have a feeling it's about to get rowdy now that the sad part is over. Caprice and Bastille did love a good knees-up, so it's only right we send them off in style. You're welcome to join us."

Rhett wrapped an arm around my shoulders. "Lead the way. They may have been in a rival gang, but we always honor the fallen."

For a shady, fallen angel, Rhett was pretty decent. I snuggled against him. It felt good not to fight my attraction for him. We were official, and I was proud to call him my guy.

As we walked into the crypt, Auntie Queenie, Lila, and Samantha followed us in.

Auntie Queenie made for the full champagne flutes and passed two glasses to me and Rhett. "Here you go, you two lovebirds. Drink up. We've got lots to get through. We've already started spending our money."

"You haven't had your payout yet," I said as I accepted a glass. "What if the Magic Council changes their mind?"

Auntie Queenie's eyes twinkled. "As if they'd dare. I'll set you on them if they do." She grinned at Rhett and patted his cheek. "Such a handsome young man." She hurried to the food-laden table where Wiggles was lurking.

"What's this about money?" Rhett asked.

"It's a long story," I said. "I'll tell you about it later."

He smiled down at me. "I look forward to it."

"Sorry I'm late." Aurora hurried through the door of the crypt. "I got caught up arranging… something."

I wasn't sure how to behave around Aurora. We'd not spoken since she'd thrown me and Wiggles out of her store.

Aurora grinned before beckoning at the door. Toby Matlock stepped through, dressed in a long dark purple velvet overcoat, a smile on his face.

"Whatever's this?" Auntie Queenie walked over. Her expression was one of suspicion as she peered at Toby. "What brings you here?"

"Queenie, always a pleasure." Toby bowed.

"Stop all that groveling nonsense. What are you doing with Aurora? This is a family party. A private celebration to remember fallen friends."

Toby's gaze cut to Rhett. "Aurora invited me."

"Aurora! I didn't realize you were friends with Toby." From the tone of Auntie Queenie's voice, she wasn't happy to see him. I couldn't say I was all that thrilled either, and the worrying way Aurora bounced on her toes made me realize she had something big planned.

"I wanted to bring you happy news," Aurora said. "I know everyone is sad about what happened to Caprice and Bastille."

"What happy news have you got to tell us?" Auntie Queenie continued to glare at Toby.

"What is it, Aurora?" Mom hurried over, followed by everyone else.

Aurora grabbed Toby's hand and smiled up at him. "I wanted you all to know that we're getting married."

The crypt erupted into chaos. Everyone talked at once, flapping around Aurora and Toby and asking dozens of questions.

Aurora smiled and blushed and gazed up at Toby.

I backed away a few steps. I wasn't happy about the news, but I wasn't surprised. Toby had been trying to convince Aurora to move in with him, and it looked like he'd taken the next step by putting a ring on her finger.

I glanced at her engagement ring finger, and my jaw dropped. She wore an enormous diamond set on a platinum band. It must have cost my annual salary and then some.

"Did you know about this?" Rhett whispered in my ear.

"I knew they were seeing each other." I tugged him away from the chaotic babble. "I had no idea about this marriage proposal."

"Toby Matlock is sly," Rhett said. "I know you think I'm shady, but that guy has some dubious history. How do they know each other?"

"That's another long story." I looked around at my family. Everyone was talking over each other, and Aurora's cheeks were bright pink, while Toby stood beside her, one arm clamped around her shoulders and his teeth gritted in a smile.

It looked like they'd be grilled for hours over this surprise announcement.

I beckoned Wiggles away from the food table and backed out of the crypt, taking Rhett with me. I couldn't deal with this today. I wasn't going to stick around and watch Aurora be quizzed about her inappropriate fiancé and how happy he made her. Their relationship didn't make me happy, but I'd already put my foot in it with Aurora and wasn't sure how to fix things.

Once we were safely away from the crypt, I looked up at Rhett. "How about that date we keep postponing? Just you and me."

"And me," Wiggles said. "I'm not hanging out with that smug, velvet covered lothario, even though the food is amazing."

Rhett grinned at Wiggles. "That's fine by me."

Wiggles nodded. "I like you. You don't have ridiculous facial hair."

"You don't want to see me grow a beard?"

"No beard!" I said. "I don't want my chin sandpapered every time I do this." I kissed his lips.

"No problem. The beard will never happen." His grip tightened around my shoulders. "What have you got in mind for our date?"

I glanced back at the crypt and winced as someone squealed. "Something quiet. Something where we can hear ourselves think."

"And somewhere that serves great food," Wiggles said.

Rhett kissed my cheek and pulled me close. "That sounds perfect. And you can tell me about your adventures in the stone circle with an assassin and why your sister is marrying Toby Matlock."

I shook my head. "That's a puzzle I've yet to solve." I would, but it was a puzzle to mull over another day.

Willow Tree Falls was safe. Esmeralda couldn't harm anyone else, and Auntie Queenie and her gang would have plenty of fun spending their money.

I took Rhett's arm as we headed out of the cemetery gates.

Right now, it was time to hang out with my two favorite guys and have some fun of our own.

About Author

K.E. O'Connor (Karen) is a cozy mystery author living in the beautiful British countryside. She loves all things mystery, animals, and cake (these feature in her books.)

When she's not writing about mysteries, murder, and treats, she volunteers at a local animal sanctuary, reads a ton of books, binge watches mystery series on TV, and dreams about living somewhere warmer.

To stay in touch with the fun mysteries, where the killer always gets caught, justice is served magic style, and the familiars talk, join her newsletter.

Newsletter:
www.subscribepage.com/cozymysteries
Website: www.keoconnor.com/writing
Facebook: www.facebook.com/keoconnorauthor

Also By

Luck of the Witch

Hell of a Witch

Revenge of the Witch

Curse of the Witch

Son of a Witch

Framing of the Witch

Trickery of the Witch

Wishes of the Witch

Harmony of the Witch

Remedy of the Witch

Gift of the Witch

Toil of the Witch

Jinxing of the Witch

Craving of the Witch

Union of the Witch

Chaos of the Witch

Sleighing of the Witch

If you enjoyed

Curse of the Witch

turn the page to read an extract from the next Crypt
Witch Mystery

SON OF A WITCH

ISBN: 978-1-915378-03-3

Chapter 1

I loved the familiar sucking pull of the magic as I slid through the barrier from the outside world back into Willow Tree Falls. It felt like home as I stood blinking in the late afternoon sunshine.

I'd only been away twenty-four hours. The demon I'd been tracking had been easy to capture. Easy but stinky.

My long hair stank like cheese that had been left on the countertop in the hot sun. And, no matter how tightly I tied the demon bag attached to my belt loop, the demon inside continued to ooze noxious fumes through the material.

I looked at my black pants and grimaced. They'd have to be burned. I doubted even my mom could remove the stench and stains on them.

Rolling my shoulders, I adjusted the bag on my hip and strolled toward Angel Force. They could deal with this pongy demon. Once they had him, I intended to kick back and enjoy a couple of lemon drops in Cloven Hoof before it got busy for the evening.

"Tempest! Tempest Crypt! Stop right there."

My shoulders hitched as I saw Mannie Winter racing toward me on his stubby legs, a bag in one hand. What did our local mayor want? We were far from friendly since I'd revealed his affair during the last mayoral election. He did nothing but glower at me and mutter whenever our paths crossed. Not this time. Mannie was smiling, and that made me suspicious.

"Phew! That's my cardio for the week." Mannie patted his round belly and blinked up at me. He was a sturdy dwarf, standing at just over five feet, with a long, well-oiled beard that trailed to his silver belt buckle.

"It looks like you need a sit down after that run," I said. "Something must be important to get you moving like that."

Mannie chuckled and smoothed his bushy eyebrows with his fingers. "Indeed, there is. I have urgent business to attend to. I haven't stopped all day."

"There's not another election coming up, is there?" Mannie had been in his role as mayor for less than a year. His vision for Willow Tree Falls was to turn it into a mecca for tourists who were attracted to our mystical stones and thermal spas. I couldn't think of anything worse than having the streets constantly thrumming with tourists. A lot of them found us anyway, but since Mannie had taken charge, the numbers had increased.

"Oh no. That's not for another four years. You're stuck with me for now." He chuckled heartily and slapped his belly.

"That's good to know. If you'll excuse me." I tried to step past him, but he matched my movement and blocked my way.

Mannie wafted his hand in front of his nose. "You've got a stinker in that bag. I hope he didn't cause you problems."

I shook the bag and more toxic fumes seeped out and wafted around Mannie. "Nothing I can't handle."

"Of course. A clever demon catching witch, such as yourself, is always in top form."

I raised my eyebrows. Why was he being so nice? "I need to be. Otherwise, I won't be alive for much longer."

Mannie chuckled again. "Absolutely. Quite right. How's the family? Is everyone keeping well?"

I wished he'd stop making small talk and tell me what he wanted. "They're all good."

"And Queenie has recovered from that terrible incident with her friends?"

"She's much better." Auntie Queenie had recently lost two of her biker gang members when one of the gang turned rogue. "She's just come back from a cruise. It's done her the world of good."

"Oh, I love a cruise," Mannie said. "There's nothing like sitting on the deck, a tankard of ale next to me and the sun on my face. Have you ever been on a cruise?"

"No. Mannie, I really must get on. This demon won't stay in the bag for much longer."

"Oh, of course. But, before you go." Mannie placed his bag on the ground and extracted a pink box with the Sprinkles bakery logo on the top. "I thought you might like a cake." He flipped the lid open to reveal a row of glistening doughnuts. There was every kind, from traditional glazed to luxuriant looking snickerdoodle.

I licked my lips. I was starving but still hesitated. Mannie Winter wanted something. All this sweet talk and now the offer of doughnuts. I raised a hand toward the doughnuts but didn't take one.

"Go on. One doughnut won't hurt." Mannie waggled his eyebrows. "You deserve it after keeping the world safe from another demon threat."

I tilted my head. "Are these treats being offered to make sure Frank doesn't come out and play with you?" Mannie knew me well, and he knew that feeding me sweet treats kept my incumbent demon from getting feisty.

Mannie shrugged and looked a little shamefaced. "It never hurts to make sure both of you are happy."

I stared at the doughnuts. They did look tasty, and you could never go wrong with a doughnut from Sprinkles.

"Wait for me!" The ground shuddered beneath my feet.

I turned to see Wiggles charging toward us, his ears flat against his head and a determined gleam in his red eyes.

My eyes widened, and I backed away. Wiggles was heading straight for the box of doughnuts in Mannie's hand. "You might like to—"

Wiggles launched into the air, colliding with the box and knocking it to the ground. He tumbled across the dirt, bounced onto his feet, and pounced on the first doughnut before it had rolled to a stop.

I sighed and looked forlornly at the fallen doughnuts.

"Well, I never." Mannie stared at the mess on the ground. "Your dog needs to go to obedience classes."

"What can I say? He's a demon when it comes to cake."

Wiggles glanced up, his mouth full of a glazed sugared doughnut. "A hellhound, actually."

Mannie glared at Wiggles as he munched on his second doughnut.

"Hey, Tempest," Wiggles said. "Good trip?"

I patted the bag. "I got the job done. Did you miss me?"

He made a muffled sound as he scooped up his next doughnut.

I took that to mean: yes, very much. And I didn't race all this way just to eat the mayor's doughnuts. I was coming to see you and tell you how happy I am that you're home.

Mannie was grumbling under his breath, his hands in fists by his sides.

"Apart from wanting to welcome me back to the village and offer me doughnuts," I said to him, "was there anything else you needed?"

"It's funny you should ask." Mannie adjusted his waistcoat. "As you know, I've been working on our exciting new tourist attraction."

My mouth twisted to the side. "The magic museum."

"It will be incredible. A history of magic and witchcraft. Dozens of exhibits, lifelike dioramas, and stunning history to enjoy. People will flock here in the thousands to see our interactive, fully immersive exhibits. I'll be unveiling a new exhibit every other month."

"I can't wait." I didn't mind a bit of history, but this museum would mean a lot more tourists, and I wasn't a fan.

"This will put us on the map." Mannie nodded. "It opens tomorrow evening. We have VIP guests and exclusive speakers attending. And we'll reveal our first exhibition. The Murder of Witches."

My eyebrows shot up. "Your first exhibit is all about how to kill my family?"

Mannie roared with laughter. "My dear Tempest, your family is indestructible. This is about the history of witch murders. The traditional methods used hundreds of years ago to hunt down witches and expose them."

I frowned. "Who wants to see that?"

"Everyone who doesn't have magic, of course," Mannie said. "There's always been a fascination from those who don't have our skills. They love to see how witches and other magical creatures were treated over the centuries."

"We were treated appallingly," I said. "Why not do a diorama about ten ways to kill irritating dwarves?"

Mannie shook his head. "No, murdering witches is all the rage."

I wouldn't mind seeing the dwarf exhibit. There was one dwarf who was tempting me to try a cruel and unusual method of killing him. "Willow Tree Falls is our haven. Why bring up the past? Here, we don't need to worry about ducking stools appearing by the pond and an angry mob with flaming torches dragging us from our beds."

"A ducking stool! It's as if you've read my mind. That's our opening exhibit."

I arched an eyebrow. "It sounds great. Best of luck with it."

"Oh, no. You misunderstand. I—"

"Mannie! Mannie! What are you doing?" A stick-thin, sharp-faced woman with a steel-gray bob strode toward Mannie, her green eyes narrowed and a pair of glasses perched on the end of her long nose.

Mannie's smile stretched across his face, but it didn't reach his eyes. "Gretel, I was about to extol your virtues to Tempest."

Gretel eyed me with suspicion. "There's no time for that. There are so many problems at the museum, I don't know where to start. You must come quickly."

Mannie chuckled, but I noticed his shoulders hunch to his ears. "Everything's running to plan. We've been over the arrangements a dozen times. It can't be anything serious." He turned to me. "Tempest Crypt, meet Gretel Le Strange. She's one of our VIP guests at the museum opening."

I nodded a greeting at Gretel. "Nice to meet you."

"Indeed." Her gaze ran over me. She wrinkled her nose when she saw the smoking bag on my hip. "What have you got there?"

"Tempest's a skilled demon hunter," Mannie said. "In fact, she has all kinds of marvelous skills."

"Good for her." Gretel turned to Mannie. "You must come at once. You have to see the disaster. If we open with the ducking stool exhibit looking like it does, we'll be a laughing stock."

"Just a moment," Mannie said. "Tempest, Gretel has been helping at the museum."

Gretel snorted. "Helping! The place would be a joke if I wasn't involved."

Mannie winced. "Gretel's a well-known historian, specializing in the history of magic."

"Congratulations," I said to her. I could do snooty too if needed.

Mannie's gaze turned anxious. "Gretel will be giving talks and demonstrations at the opening tomorrow."

I nodded and watched Wiggles with envy as he polished off the dirt-covered doughnuts. He would have such bad indigestion. I wouldn't be sharing a bed with him tonight.

"Since we're having VIP visitors at the museum," Mannie continued, "I'm in need of your expertise."

I glanced at him. "To do what?"

"To assist with the security. It's such an important event, and the place will be crammed full of guests."

"Okay, but it's a museum. Why do you need security?"

"Because of our important guests." Mannie tilted his head at Gretel, who stood tapping her foot. "Along with Gretel, we also have the author of the book who helped bring this museum to life."

Gretel snorted. "Isadora might have written some popular piece of fluff about the history of witchcraft, but it's hardly instrumental in creating the museum. In case you've forgotten, I've advised you every day for nine months on this matter."

Mannie's lips pressed together. "I haven't forgotten. Your input has been most welcome."

Gretel huffed and folded her arms across her chest. "We need to get a move on. Stop wasting your time with this witch."

"Tempest is going to help us," Mannie said, a pleading look entering his eyes. "I need her for the extra security at the museum."

I shook my head. "I'm no security expert. Why don't you ask the angels?"

Mannie scuffed a foot in the dirt. "The angels are lovely creatures, and they do their best. I'm not sure they can handle a security job of such importance. Things could get hectic. What if someone needs calming down?"

"Have you ever been hit in the face with an angel wing? They sting. It would calm anyone down." I didn't want anything to do with this. "If your museum guests get rowdy after their sherry, the angels can handle them. I don't run a security team."

"You've got experience from running Cloven Hoof," Mannie said. "You have door staff."

"What's Cloven Hoof?" Gretel sneered. "It sounds like some disreputable devil's den, a place for down and outs."

"You're pretty close." My smile felt more like a snarl. "We have a specific clientele we cater to."

"I doubt I'd enjoy your establishment," Gretel said.

"It's definitely not for you." My fingers flexed, and I took a step closer to Gretel.

Mannie grabbed my arm. "Please, Tempest, I need the very best for our guests. Whatever you need to make it a success, it's yours."

I pulled my arm from his grasp. "I need nothing. I'm not a bouncer. This isn't what I do."

"Money's no object."

Gretel scowled at Mannie and turned away from us, her foot continuing to beat on the ground.

Mannie leaned closer. "Please, Gretel's very demanding. I need somebody to keep an eye on her and make sure she doesn't take over and spoil things."

I stepped away from him and studied Gretel's back. She did look like a handful, but I didn't want to hang out with a rude magic historian for an evening.

"Try someone else. Rhett's gang is always good if you're looking for muscle to keep things under control."

"Oh, no. They're not the right kind of security." Mannie shook his head swiftly. "You can handle yourself in a professional manner if there's trouble." He nodded at the bag on my hip, which now oozed a green sludge from the bottom. "You look after the demons. You even have your own under control these days."

Gretel spun on her chunky-heeled shoes and scowled at me. "You own a demon?"

I shook my head. "No. It's a long story."

"There'll be canapés and champagne. You'd be free to help yourself," Mannie said. "You'll be doing me such a favor."

"Did someone say free canapés?" Wiggles belched out smoke, which was tinged with the smell of sulfur.

Gretel took several steps back and pinched her nose.

"Sorry, Mannie. I'm out. You'll have to find someone else."

He caught hold of my elbow, and his eyes glittered. "I wasn't going to mention this, but if you do this for me, last month's noise violation will disappear. What do you say? The paperwork vanishes, you get a decent bit of cash in your pocket, and you can drink and eat 'til your heart's content."

This time, it was my turn to scowl. That noise violation would cost me a few thousand in fines, and there was no way out of it. "Just one evening?"

"That's all I ask. Get there at six, and we'll be done by eleven."

I rubbed my forehead, not happy with Mannie's underhanded tactics. "Can I bring an extra body? Suki looks after the door at Cloven Hoof most nights. She's good at keeping order."

"Absolutely, bring whoever you like," Mannie said. "Same goes for them, free canapés and drinks."

"I'd better get out my smart bowtie," Wiggles said, "if I'm going to be a bouncer for the evening."

Mannie blinked at Wiggles before nodding. "Why not? A hellhound as security will be a fun bonus."

Wiggles strutted around us. "I'll take my payment in bones and cupcakes."

I sighed. It looked like I'd be adding bouncer to my resume. "We'll be there."

"That's excellent news." Mannie smiled at me before turning to Gretel, whose face looked set in a permanent frown.

"My time is precious," she snapped at him.

"Of course." Mannie nodded at Gretel. "Let's see about this museum exhibit you're not happy with."

I watched them walk away. "How were the doughnuts?" I asked Wiggles.

"Tasty. A bit gritty, but they were free."

"They looked lovely. Maybe save me one the next time you knock a whole box on the ground."

"You wouldn't have liked them. Some had coconut sprinkles on the top."

I stuck my tongue out. I wasn't a big coconut fan. "Come on. Let's get rid of this demon. Then we need to figure out how we're going to avoid falling asleep at this dull museum opening."

Wiggles nudged me with his nose as we walked to Angel Force. "It's good to have you back. I sort of miss you when you're not around."

I smiled down at him. "I missed you too, you greedy hellhound."

Son of a Witch is available in paperback and e-book.

ISBN: 978-1-915378-03-3